Wide Awake

WIDE AWAKE

Kristin Beale

NEW YORK

LONDON • NASHVILLE • MELBOURNE • VANCOUVER

Wide Awake

Published in New York, New York, by Morgan James Publishing. Morgan James is a trademark of Morgan James, LLC. www.MorganJamesPublishing.com

Proudly distributed by Ingram Publisher Services.

ISBN 9781636980867 paperback
ISBN 9781636980874 ebook
Library of Congress Control Number: 2022948365

Cover Design by:
Andy Magee
amdesigner.co.uk

Interior Design by:
Christopher Kirk
www.GFSstudio.com

Thank you to my husband, Christopher,
who listened to me talk about tampons for way too long.

And to my mother, who begged me to take that chapter out.

Frieda

My name is Frieda, but I've been called a lot of other names in my life. Freida is the name I'm most comfortable in, though, because I'm not a boy. Life is short, and there's no time to be uncomfortable. But I don't think my name much matters to anyone except me.

I'm pretty laid back about most things, but I'm not happy about where I am right now. I haven't really liked the places I was before this either, though, so I guess I've never really been happy. Not *really*. Am I whining? I don't care. Maybe I'm also a whiner.

I grew up in a patch surrounded by my like. It was good to be with my family—I guess that's what we'll call them—but I also didn't really care. They don't matter. Even though we were all basically the same, we didn't talk much in there. Or, really, at all. There wasn't anything to talk about because none of us knew anything about who or what was coming, so it's not like we felt close to each other. I was alone on that dirt just as much as I'm alone next to the step of this porch. I think I'm probably better off this way. Alone. It's what I'm used to.

My days lying in the patch were long and ran together, but where I am now is actually taking time off my life. Sitting next to the third step, I can feel my once bright, orange casing wrinkling and darkening and my inside skin growing soft. I feel naked. Empty.

I remember my last day in the patch—the day I was chosen—like it just happened. The sunlight of the afternoon had only just started to drop, and the temperature was getting evening-low. All kinds were walking up and down our rows: short, taller, skinny, heavier. Honestly, they all ran together after a while. I think they came to our rows to judge and find their favorite. I looked forward to when they came, and I wanted to be found. The nights were coming earlier, the weather growing colder, and the wind pricked the top of my head. It wasn't the most *comfortable* thing, not really, but those changes also meant that visits from the short, tall, skinny, and fat were a tradition of my evenings.

I didn't mind their stomping through and disturbing our dirt so much, mostly because it was something different. I lay in the dirt, alone with my thoughts and minding my business all day, so I welcomed any kind of distraction. The biggest reason I preferred the distracted peace of my daytime in the patch was that I could count on a busy evening to follow. When I think back on it now, I'd choose a hundred endless and chaotic daytimes over what I went through when I left that place. But back then, I didn't know what I do now, so I was always looking for the next thing, the next action, instead of enjoying the peace that was already there.

Two people—a girl and a boy—came to me one evening just as the sun started to set. They were all smiles and hand-holding when they walked up, until the girl disappeared behind me to grab, *kidnap*, me from the dirt. I remember these details clearly because she scared the seeds out of me.

Well, not literally. Not yet anyway.

The girl, her hands steady on my sides, heaved me off the ground, then spun me around a few times. She was stronger than I expected, which I appreciated, but that just made my physical exam more terrifying. By no means was I ready for it, either. Of course I wasn't. Her face was a blur as she spun me around, so I couldn't take any clues on what she was thinking. I guess I was good enough because when I stopped spinning, she had a long smile across that face of hers.

She said something to the boy, and they laughed together, carrying me away from my home in the dirt for the first and the last time. They grinned as we walked through the patch of my family, so I assumed they were together. I thought they were a couple, a happy one. I remember how happy I was to be going to a good home.

To be clear: they chose me as their favorite of all the others in the patch. Their favorite out of *hundreds*. I should have felt honored, flattered, and respected. I didn't, not really. Mostly, I was uncomfortable and a little nervous. My life in the patch was predictable. When I left it, I had no clue what was next. Only in hindsight did I realize I'd never be back in that dirt, and all that movement was me going "home." My new home.

After hours, it seemed, of tossing and rolling around, my movement stopped. The chaos of the tossing and rolling meant I hadn't had any capacity to reflect on what had happened to me, and what was happening. The stillness didn't last long, though; seconds after I had my first moment of peace, my movement started again. And all at once. One final jerk from the girl, then one final spin. I couldn't even really process my discomfort because she kept going. She dropped me into my next situation, never softly enough. My new spot was alongside the bottom step of some porch. Only heaven knows where. I was miles away from the familiarity of my dirt patch, though. That much I knew.

I couldn't tell it then, but I'd be sitting in that spot for a long time—much longer than I anticipated. I don't know how much time I spent waiting, but if I had to guess, I'd say at least a month. Maybe two. Every day looks and feels the same to me. I'm a pumpkin. You can't expect me to keep track of this stuff.

Time passed slowly, and that's what it felt like: two months. For a long time, I thought my spot next to the step was part of my destiny: to sit until The Rot came. I had imagined bigger things for myself, so I can't say that possibility didn't disappoint. But my feelings don't make much difference.

I watched her walk past me so many times in those felt-like-two months that I thought she had forgotten about me completely. That spoke to an insecurity I dreamed up in the patch: I'm not round enough, plump enough, or *pumpkin* enough. Whatever that means. Everything that preceded the girl taking me home and forgetting me on that step only confirmed those insecurities. I had a lot of time to sit and reflect on my situation so, eventually, my unhappiness turned to despondency. As I am, my hope is pretty much all I have. And my hope was almost gone.

I spent a lot of time in my thoughts back then, so I jumped to all sorts of conclusions. As you can imagine, being forgotten was a mighty disservice to my self-image. It's not that I was in any physical danger while I waited, but I certainly felt the dread of it. There was no mystery of how my story would end. I'd seen what happened to the others once they left their dirt in the patch, so I knew what to expect: she would carve me, cut me up, then set me on display for The Rot to come and for the world to watch. I knew I'd probably get a smile or similar-feeling shape carved into my face, and I suspected it wouldn't be entirely sincere. But I guess I just thought I'd be happier by that point. I didn't think a smile would be as much of a far fetch.

You all know how this Jack O' Lantern business works, so you know how right I was about it all. My fate on the porch and my dying in the open was a public execution, but I didn't expect the other *monstrous* stuff that had to happen before I got to that point. I had no choice but to go along with it all, too . . . with a smile on my face.

The worst part of everything that happened—even over the scraping and cutting—was the humiliation. The degradation. In my darkest hours, the hope I held onto was that my lines were even and my circles rounded. But even I knew that was a lot to hope for.

Let's not skip ahead.

The girl came to visit me on that first step from time to time. *Praise be.* I thought I might be spending the rest of my life there so, even more than when I was taken from the patch, I had no idea what to expect. She came to me during the day to sit on the step alongside me, and it felt good. We clicked. For the first time since I left my dirt, I thought I was where I needed to be. Sometimes, she would come to me to cry and sometimes to talk on the phone, but mostly, she just sat. I didn't see the boy around much after that first night; she was always alone when we hung out, so maybe he wasn't her romance like I had thought. That might have been another of my jumps, but who knows?

I don't know who that boy was to her, but it would have been nice to see him again, if only for the fact of how happy they seemed. My selfish part wanted him back because I had already lost my family, my dirt, and my "comfort-ability" when I left that patch. I didn't feel like I could lose something else—him—on top of that. But that might be my insecurity talking.

I waited on that step for a long time. At least that's how it felt. But I was learning while I waited. I learned about the rain, about the neighborhood, and about the two of them. My new home had more for me to watch than my home in the patch, so that's what I did all day; I watched, and I soaked it up. I watched the neighborhood kids playing in the street, and I learned the nights are heaps colder than the days, and I understood that the two of them weren't as happy as I'd first thought. Now that I was over the hump of leaving my family in the patch, my dreams matured to leaving my spot by the porch for the warm inside, alongside them. The boy left the scene pretty soon after we unloaded the car that first day, and he didn't come back. None of my dreams came true. It's okay.

I waited for two weeks, maybe three, before the boy bounded past me and up the steps without even a glance in my direction. What followed were some loud shouts back and forth, the sound of her tears (I think that's what that was), then silence. The silence was the worst part because I had no idea what was going on. Or what he did. How she was.

That situation repeated a couple more times in the following weeks, and I used his coming and going as a distraction from myself and my own troubles. I didn't give much thought to what was happening *to* me because there was so much happening *around* me. The last time he left, he didn't come back for a long time, and there was silence. So much silence. And that's when all the questions and all the awareness caught up to me:

What was I doing there?

Why was I still on the step?

What was going to happen to me?

I'd been using those questions as distractions to avoid having to process them all. But when they fell silent, I had no choice but to focus on myself. My destiny.

I watched the pumpkins sitting on neighboring steps around mine and tried to take a hint of what was coming for me. They were in all stages, from virgin and untouched (like me), gutted and drained, carved with a smile, and rotting. *The Rot.* I was surrounded by what I guessed was a timeline of what was to come. Of her options. I grouped them into two categories: complete and undone. In my mind, my virgin and smiling friends were at their final stage, and the gutted then uncarved were unfinished jobs. Those were the Undones.

I didn't wish to be cut open, not really, but I could appreciate the integrity of my virginity, and the finality of my smiling peers. Where we had an intention, the Undones had a stunted effort. Truly, I thought I would take my virginity to the Rot. I was very wrong, but it was okay. I never really felt one way or the other about it—no fear, no excitement, no apprehension, nothing. It's not like my feelings would have changed anything, anyway.

The girl came to me one day for what I thought was another cry. She didn't sit down next to me, but she stood in front, wrapped her hands around my fattest parts, and lifted me from the ground. This lift felt less like a kidnapping, but it was no less terrifying. She walked me up the steps—more tossing than I was used to—and carried me through what I guessed was her house. Everything was new to me, but I hardly had the time to appreciate it. We walked through her house to a large room, where she set me on a table. I could hardly keep up with what was happening, except to think it might be a step toward putting that smile on my face. I wouldn't be dying a virgin, after all.

She stared at me for a minute longer—similar to how she stared at me that first day in the patch—then pulled a pen out from somewhere. I guessed the pen was for her to either decide or let me in on her vision for what I'd look like at the end of my reconstruction. I was kinda excited about it. She could make me into anything, really: a witch on a broomstick, a cat, a screaming face, a flower, anything. I guessed the process of drawing her plan on my skin would be uncomfortable, but I also hoped that my anticipation would make it not so bad. Again, my hope was all I had.

I was wrong about some things. To my delight, the pen rolling over my rind tickled a bit, like nothing I'd ever felt. Not in a bad way. I didn't mind it. She drew lines, then traced over those lines once, twice, three times. Perhaps no surprise, because that's how this stuff goes: the odd, ticklish feeling went away after her first draft. Then the pressure grew more unpleasant with every outline. Judging from the perfectionism and force she used to draw those lines and shapes, I guessed she was trying to create a perfect stencil to trace and guide her cuts later on.

Someone, please tell that girl that no one is going to see her pen lines, ever, no matter how perfect and straight they are. Save the next pumpkin some pain.

The most intense and awful part came next, so it feels petty to even mention the stencil. The hollowing. I knew the cutting and slicing parts would happen, but I had no idea that to cut me up, the entirety of my inside flesh needed to be scraped, scooped, and separated from my body by way of a circular hole from the top of my head. Bring it on, I guess.

The girl, who I'll now call my *executioner*, pulled out an unnecessarily sharp blade to slash a hole through my top. That part actually wasn't as bad as it sounds; I guess I don't have as many nerve endings up there. She cut that circle in my head, tore my stem from it, and I started to relax in my becoming callous to it all. In hindsight, that was the last time I was able to relax. At least until another lifetime.

She stuck her warm, white hand through that circular hole in my top to pull out my guts, my seeds, and my soul. She jerked them out so hard, I thought she might be holding a grudge against me, *a pumpkin*. That she stole my seeds was the worst part of all, though, because losing them meant losing a part of my future. Without my seeds, I have no hope of reproducing. Her hand guaranteed the end of my line, and that felt personal. The hollowing slammed me with not only the discomfort of my insides being yanked out but also with a truckload of psychological distress. Everything all at once.

She dragged my seeds out anyway, despite how I felt about it, and she dropped them into a pile next to where I sat. It was humiliating, you can imagine, but that didn't register right away; I was so preoccupied with the loss of my seeds that I couldn't make sense of much more. My whole body throbbed from the shock and pain of the extraction, which, in hindsight, I wish those feelings were ones that didn't register instead of the humiliation. My pain had a heartbeat, but the vicious kind.

Everything all at once felt unbearable, and I've already tried to bury my feelings around this. Because what good are they? I don't have a choice but to sit with them. I'm trying to move on. I'm trying. But it isn't easy. Nothing about this is easy.

I expected the next thing that happened, the cutting, but I didn't expect how I would already feel when I got there: broken, reduced, empty. After the hollowing, I could feel myself fading—either from the physical pain of it or from the anticipation of my body being slashed apart chunk by chunk. My feelings don't make a difference, remember, so she went right into it. Chunk by chunk.

The first cut was the worst. You may know this, but nothing about carving a pumpkin is quick or easy. That first penetration was the hardest for me, I think because the flesh—my flesh—had to be broken. I knew it was coming, and I was wrong about my awareness making the pain any easier. No matter how eyes-open you are, I don't think anyone can really be *ready* for that kind of thing. That cut felt like a punch in the stomach—except it was a steak knife, and it was my head.

Once she made the first cut, I had no choice but to be present for it all; I was aware of and sensitive to every slash, slice, and scrape of that blade on my insides and outside my flesh. Aside from the shooting pain of that initial piercing, the rest of the cuts were constant in their sting. That is to say, they didn't get any less painful. I never grew numb to any of it.

I'm done with the cutting and the torture now, as I'm telling you this, and I still don't know what I look like. Or if I even turned out how she expected. But I'm confident it's right—she took too much care for me not to look right, and I don't think she would have left me alone if I was anything short. I just feel drained. *Dizzy.* I let myself fade in and out while she cut my body to pieces and scraped my incisions over and over with her blade. She was meticulous in every step of my carving, so I know I at least look clean and my lines are straight. Her cuts were like her lines of planning: not finalized until they were scraped and shaved to perfection. In the cutting stage, perfectionism looks like scraping over the same path repeatedly, as if her mother's life depended on their integrity. At that point, her perfectionism shouldn't have come as a surprise, but somehow, it did. It was an *unwelcome* surprise, I don't need to say.

Like the cuts, the knife's scraping was something I couldn't be ready for. Imagine dragging a potato peeler over a fresh wound: back and forth, back and forth. I appreciated her thoroughness in the beginning—I really did. After the pen's stabbing, the seed and gut-jerking, and the carving, though, I wholly stopped caring about my accuracy and neatness, and I was only focused on getting it over with. I'm a pumpkin, not a painting. I just wanted it over with.

And finally, it was. I've accepted that I'll probably never see what I look like, but I felt every step of it, so I have a rough idea. I know I have holes for eyes, and I know those holes are round based on how much she scraped to make them so. I know I have a long mouth oriented upward to emulate a smile. I have a small hole under my eyes where a nose should be, and she only scraped those edges through twice. On my backside, toward my bottom, she carved her initials, "MEA," in block letters. Those cuts were smaller, and they were quick but, by the nature of them, just as excruciating. No rest for the wicked.

Here's the only thing I was right about: my smile is entirely fake. I'm long past any kind of happiness.

So here we are. That's everything that has happened to this point, and now you see where I'm coming from. The last stop, and it feels like the last stop, is to clean up. I think that's what I'm sitting here for, what I'm waiting on.

If I thought I was fading before—and I did—then I don't know what to call myself now. *Deadened*. My pulp is sagging to the outside of my body, and my wounds are raw—perfectly shaped, but raw. I must look paralyzed and ridiculous, but I also know it could be worse; at least my lines are straight and my holes round. There's some dignity left.

"Almost done," she spoke, even if under her breath, for the first time. Her voice was soft and almost sympathetic as she wiped a wet cloth over my body to move my guts away. She squeezed and rubbed a clear gel over my orange skin, what was left of it, and hummed something about making me "last." The gel was cold on my flesh, and it shocked me . . . but in a good way. Her hands were soft as she spread the gel around—evenly and slowly—until my orange was covered. I appreciated her in those moments, perhaps for the first time since she took me from the patch.

As suddenly as her dropping me next to the step, which feels like a year ago, her hands stopped moving, and she was gone. I was alone again, *at last*. Everything I'd been through until that moment was a hardship: the kidnapping, the hollowing, the carving, even the gelling. Then, after all that, she's gone, and I'm back on the step. But I'm a different pumpkin.

This second time around is different because this time, I'm naked, hollowed out, and slippery. The cold wind is flowing through my body and escaping through my holes, but I feel okay. The passing of time has dulled my memory enough that I can think back on everything I've been through and feel some kind of peace about it all; most of the pain and shock have faded to my memory, so I think back and feel almost grateful for it. All that suffering has brought me to where I am, at this point, which is resting and possibly stronger, with all the pain and injury behind me.

Now, after all I've been through since the patch, my body feels like the hours after a hard workout. I still kinda hurt and my surface area is still throbbing, but it's over. The pain is over, and I can relax in that. I don't know how much time has passed since I was taken from my dirt patch, and I don't know how much longer I can last until The Rot takes over, but I'm thankful to be resting and feeling "pruned." I expect that gel she covered me with will hold off The Rot for a few extra days, but it's still coming. So I'm just trying to enjoy where I am, while I can.

When I don't look good anymore and I start to expire, on to the next things: The Rot and the garbage. I watched the neighborhood pumpkins while I was on the first step, and I got a little idea of what the Rot looks like. I've heard a little about it from other pumpkins in the patch, too, and I'm curious if it'll be as fun as it sounds. I'll sit on this step until it comes for me, though, enjoying my slippery skin and the wind running through me. Really, it's not so bad. I'm content sitting here, at least, and that's the first time I can say as much.

Tuesday, October 22

I've been single most of my life, which is fine. It's probably better that way. I like my independence, and I like doing things a particular way, so being on my own works out. A boyfriend has never been something I've thought about and hoped for like most of the girls I know. It just isn't. My life has been the *Madison Show*, hosted by yours truly. I've enjoyed every minute of it.

Well, okay. *Almost* every minute.

I'm saying "almost" because there are some parts of a boyfriend that I'd like to have, especially at this time of the year: a date for holiday parties, someone to do silly traditions with (carve pumpkins, wear matching pajamas, build a cookie house), and an ear to listen when I have a bad day. You know what I'm saying: I don't *need* a boyfriend, but there are times it would be nice. The reason I'm single isn't that I haven't been interested in anyone, either. I have, but just not with anyone who reciprocates. It's fine. I try not to internalize that part.

None of that matters now, though, because someone is finally interested in me. It feels really good. I'm excited about him, but it's a sensation like I'm jumping headfirst into a pool that my peers have been swimming in since high school, and I've only just bought a swimsuit. Meaning, I've never been romantically involved with anyone, and I have no clue what I'm doing. I'm jumping into the metaphorical deep end at the same time I'm learning how to swim.

The guy who's interested in me is named Charlie. As in, Charlie from math class, third block, junior year of high school. More than a decade ago. I sat next to him at the back of the class for the whole semester, and he flirted with me first. I didn't really know how to give it back, but whatever I did, left an impression because he recognized me all these years later.

I ran into Charlie, literally *into* him, when I was rushing out the door of that coffee shop by my parents' house. I spilled my freakin' tea on the guy, and he still asked for my number. I figured that one morning had used all my good luck for the year, but then he sent me a message the next day and asked for a first date. So maybe there's no such thing as a luck quota.

Getting to know Charlie as an adult, he's the kind of person who can drive me crazy and at the same time, he's like a drug I can't get enough of. Not a ton has changed since high school-he was irresistible in that same frustrating way back then too. We've been in and out of a relationship since our coffee shop run-in, but none of it has felt very serious because we keep going out again. Mostly, we're in I guess.

If it was the other way around, I'd have an easier time getting off this on-then-off-again roller coaster we're riding. When Charlie and I are good, we're so good. But when we're bad, it's like a hangover.

Our relationship is complicated, but I think Charlie and I love each other. It's not something either of us has said out loud yet. Most of the time, that's just how it feels. That's the "so good" part. But then, when the flip switches, we can hardly stand to be in the same room. *He* can't stand to be in the same room with *me*, to be accurate. Our relationship is complicated, but sometimes, it can be really good. Those are the highs that keep me coming back.

There are some things that Charlie doesn't like about me, but I get it. I look for things about him I don't like just as much, but I guess I'm still in the "Honeymoon Stage." I've justified and taken the weight of every negativity he has thrown at me so far, which leaves him clean as a carrot.

He's yelling at me, but I probably deserve that. Why can't I be better for him?

We get in arguments over stupid stuff. I should be able to calm him down so he can let it go.

Charlie is mad again. I'm not a good girlfriend. I suck at this.

He doesn't know a lot of things about me, but I've never let anyone in that far, so I can't expect him to. It's okay. Nobody understands everything about another person, I don't think, so it makes sense that Charlie gets impatient sometimes. I can be overwhelming, and his way of dealing is to walk away. I don't know what he's capable of when he gets to the top of his frustration, so I'd maybe even prefer that he walk away. Charlie is like a drug to me, and that comes with some immunity and lots of my justification. He gets away with things because I'm addicted to him. An addict of a different sort.

Fall is the perfect time of year for Charlie and me. Every year, I see my friends posting idiotic pictures with their boyfriends, doing silly holiday traditions, and dressing up in goofy costumes. Please believe that I'm the one to roll my eyes the hardest at those people. But now that I have Charlie, it's my turn.

Charlie and I have already been to the pumpkin patch, and we picked a pumpkin to carve together. This one will be our first holiday as a pair-hopefully, one of many-and pumpkin carving will be our first cringey tradition. In my head, it was all going to be cute, fun, and probably romantic.

In hindsight, I was off with the "romantic" and "cute" adjectives, but it did start off fun. Cringey, yes, but in a different way than what I had hoped.

We picked a chilly afternoon to go to the pumpkin patch. I remember that detail because I wore a sweater I thought I looked good in, and I was excited for him to see me in it. I was hoping for something cheesy like him wrapping me in his arms to keep me warm. But I was also playing it cool. In the beginning, I played "the Game." Mom talked me through it before I left for our first date: make him work for my attention and play a little "hard to get." I tried to play, I really did, but I don't think I was any good at it. Something I was doing was working for us, though, because we were happy back then.

There were a lot of other people at the patch the night we went. We chased, walked alongside, or held hands down every row, searching for our favorite. We looked at every blasted pumpkin in that patch until the sun went down and the night went from "chilly" to "plain cold." Charlie had a way of making everything fun-even the monotonous stuff.

He saw a pumpkin he liked first, and even said was "perfect." I'm not even sure what that means-it looked like all the other pumpkins to me. He might have just said he liked it because he was tired of searching, or maybe there really was something special about it. I certainly didn't see its novelty, but you'd never know it. I picked up that pumpkin like it was made of gold. I held it in my hands, spun it around a few times, and bunched my lips to judge it. I was acting a part-either silly and playing along or serious and considering, I don't know. I was still figuring him out and how to act with him. We had lots of fun together, and I enjoyed being around him. I *enjoy* being around him.

Good things never last, I guess.

Charlie and I got into a fight in the car on the way home, believe it or not. He was frustrated about something I did, but I can't even remember what. I can't forget how quickly it elevated, though. It scared me not for my safety, but because it felt foreboding.

It's just the learning curve, I remember thinking. Every relationship has one. My relationship history is scattered with more of the same story: he gets frustrated about something I do or some way I act; I try to change to fit into his mold, and we still break up soon after. Charlie's frustration that night just about sent me into a panic. I really wanted us to last.

Like in all new relationships, both people have to learn to take the good parts with the bad. My "bad" just looks a little different from other people's "bad." I needed Charlie to be patient with me, but he couldn't. He *wouldn't,* and that's what broke us. When he was frustrated, he was cruel. When he lost his patience, he said very unkind things. I tried to show grace when he acted like a monster. I know I can be a lot sometimes, but he wasn't giving it in return. In the end,

Charlie broke up with me before we even got to carve his "perfect" pumpkin.

He left the pumpkin here, at my apartment, so I was stuck with its perfection on my front step. I was reminded of Charlie and of our breakup every time I passed it, but it was a pain I felt like I *should* feel. At least for a little while. And in the beginning, I let it swallow me. I sat on the step with his "perfect" pumpkin and thought about Charlie. The pumpkin was my way of feeling closer to him, I guess. I'm not going to pretend like I didn't cry most of the time I sat with it, but I also felt like I *should*. I saw it as a punishment for letting him slip away from me. I felt so bad about myself, so low. I wanted back the cheesy holiday couple that bounced up and down the rows at the pumpkin patch. However silly, I started to see that pumpkin as our bridge back to the happiness of when we picked it from the patch.

I carried on like that for two weeks. Two weeks of my entire weakness is what I needed, I guess, before I could find the motivation to do something with it: either rewrite the memories tied to it (carve it myself) or throw it away (let it beat me). One thing I couldn't do was let the pumpkin live on my front porch anymore, hoping Charlie would miss me, we'd work out our differences, and he'd want to carve it like we'd planned. I had to get rid of it so I could start to move on.

Charlie was my first real boyfriend, and I wanted it to last forever. I thought we might. I've been on my own for most of my life, so I well know how to be, but it just took me a few weeks to get back to it. Leaving the pumpkin untouched to rot on my front step contradicted all my healing, though, and throwing it away felt like a defeat. However corny, I wanted to reclaim the memories attached to the pumpkin and make them *mine.* So I made a plan. Step one was to carve the pumpkin *by myself* and enjoy doing it. There's my revenge.

I had a plan for how I wanted our pumpkin to look: a nice-looking face with a happy smile. Typical pumpkin behavior. I stuck to that plan, despite what was reflecting from my heart-something more sinister and more indicative of how I was feeling about being single again. Alone, still. A part of me would have liked to carve *Charlie's* face instead of his "perfect" pumpkin. If I could, I'd give him a permanent smile so he wouldn't have a choice but to be happy and patient with me. I would carve him the same smile I'd spent so much time chasing after.

In the end, though, I followed the plan for a happy-seeming pumpkin-in case Charlie ever came by and saw the carved product. I wanted him to see its smile and realize that I'm okay without him.

I *am* okay without him, but I didn't feel okay for a while.

I carved a smile, but I must have cried for half the time it took to finish it. My tears turned to anger by the time I finished drawing my outline, causing me to maybe push too hard on the pen. Then, when I plunged my hand in it to rip the guts away from its rind, that's when it started to feel good-the kind of *good* that happens when you have a knife in your hands. I took my anger out by ripping its guts and seeds. I cried while I cut through its skin, then I smoothed the edges of my heartache with a blade. I rode my anger's roller coaster with a pumpkin instead of with a person so, in that way, my jack-o'-lantern was my therapist.

I scraped, shaved, and scratched over all my cuts until every line and every hole was exact. A little of that perfectionism came from a place of indignance, but mostly, I just wanted my pumpkin to look good. So I didn't stop until it did. That's one of the things that drove Charlie crazy about me. I "don't know when to give up." But I call it an asset.

Those were the words he yelled before he left my house that night, along with some other things. Charlie could be cruel. No one had ever brought my "flaws" to the spotlight quite like Charlie did, so hearing them was a shock-almost as much as a wound. I had never been in a *real* relationship before him, so the things he yelled at me were ones I had grown blind to. The part that surprised and stung me the most was how he used my routines against me as articles of war. Charlie's anger is part of the reason I've been single for most of my life. It's just easier.

I named my pumpkin Jack. He had two eyes, one small nose, and a wide grin. I thought a nose was a funny thing to put on a pumpkin, so that was my touch. Jack was one-of-a-kind, like me. I carved my initials on Jack's backside so he would know that he's mine, and I'll never abandon him like Charlie did me. In hindsight, that part is kinda silly. With all the symbolism and the emotional roller coaster I rode to carve him, though, I was feeling sentimental. I'm not usually the type, but I was a mess.

I carved Jack a goofy-looking smile, sliced his edges to flawless, and healed my broken heart a little in the process. The last step in my pumpkin therapy was something I read about online: cover it in petroleum jelly to make it last longer. I wanted Jack to be around for a while as a reminder of what I can do without Charlie . . . and so he would see Jack when he came around to apologize. I wanted Jack to last longer than most pumpkins, and I think that's understandable. So I jellied him up.

"Almost done," I whispered to myself, or to the pumpkin, as I wiped a wet cloth over his body. I was talking to the pumpkin and cleaning his guts like a poopy baby out of a bath. I realize that. I'm not a loony-I was in a different way.

"This will make you last," I whispered softly as I rubbed the jelly over his surface.

BLING . . . BRIIING . . .

BLING . . . BRIIING . . .

My phone's ringtone is either the most jarring or the most exhilarating noise, depending on what's going on in my head at that moment. I was in a pumpkin trance when it rang, so this time it jarred me. But the exhilaration caught me right after.

What if it's Charlie?

Maybe he has regrets?

He wants me back?

I put the pumpkin down on the step and shot over to my phone. I was hoping it was Charlie, and I was ready to play *cool* if it was: maybe answer on the third ring, or yell, "I'll be right there!" to the empty room before telling him I had to go. Or maybe I'd let it go to voicemail, then call him back in a few hours. Remember the Game.

The Game I played at the beginning of my and Charlie's relationship was a different kind. I was on a different level back then. Then was the "Getting To Know You, But Also Getting You To Like Me" game. Now, after his declaration that I'm "frustrating" and I can be "too much," the Game has hit a different level of *cool*: a new set of rules and totally different gameplay.

All the planning and forethought I'm giving to this thing, whatever it is, with Charlie is stressful and even feels a little pathetic. But I guess that's how relationships can sometimes be. I'm new to this. The stress and the *sad* will pay off one day, I hope. When we get back to how we used to be. Still, I'd choose the drama of Charlie over the loneliness and grief of my solitude.

I hope writing my feelings in this journal will help me process everything a little better. The internet named keeping a journal and "tuning into yourself" as the first step of healing after a breakup, so here's my shot. I'm trying to be better. I know it might not sound like it, but we used to be happy. And we can get back to that. I know we can. How I feel now, I'll do what it takes to get my Charlie back.

Oscar

My name is Oscar, and I hang in a dining room. Somewhere. I don't know where the room is or how long I've been here because those details don't matter much, do they? It's not like I can change anything. I remember a little about what I look like from when I was made, though, so there's something. Here's what I know:

I'm a painting of a barn—a bright red one with white doors and a white roof. The barn is on a green field surrounded by tall trees and a light blue sky. I think there are clouds. I don't remember any people in my painting, but I'm okay with that because I'd rather you focus on my scenery than the lives of fictional strangers. I guess I'd be happy either way, though, so long as someone is looking at me. My memory has preserved the vibrant colors of the day I was created, but I sometimes wonder what I look like now. What feels like a hundred years later. The artist who painted me was sharing his memory of a place I've still never been to, and I'm not even sure exists in real life.

I can only hope my colors are as vibrant and I look as good as I did on day one. My paint strokes used to be clean and sharp, but there's no telling what I look like now. Back then, I was a replication of his memory, if not an exact copy. These days, I'm probably a color-faded and oilier version. I haven't seen myself since that first day, so those are just my assumptions. A bit of me wonders what I look like now, but a larger bit would rather keep that memory in its perfect form. I just don't want to be disappointed.

I know what this room is that I'm hanging in, and I have an idea of what I look like, but I don't know much more. I know the girl that owns me, Madison, and I've gathered that one more person is living here with her. A boy. I've seen him walking around, and he's almost as attractive as she is. They look good together. I don't see much outside this room because it's not in the middle of the action like in my last house, but I think I have enough context. I prefer in here where I'm removed from the goings-on, anyway. I don't mind the solitude. Really.

I was hung high in the living room of the last house I was in—the owners before Madison—and I saw everything: people coming and going, the commotion of their every day, and what they did when they thought nobody was watching. In this room, though, I'm disconnected from it all; there isn't as much for me to see or listen to. It's not as fun, maybe, but my disconnection also means nobody touches me. So it's a fair trade. The dining room can be boring and too quiet sometimes, but the isolation is worth my sacrifice. Nobody touches me in here.

It's not like anyone asked me where in the house I wanted to be hung, but I'm just saying.

I enjoyed hanging in the living room, the middle of it all, but I paid a price. Over time, the surface of my paint became grimy from the obligatory fingerprints that come from hanging at an arm's distance. And there was that sacrifice for centrality. The living room was the nucleus of that house, and the reason I was there in the first place was to make it look nice. It was an honor, really, and my privilege. I don't think anyone would hang me in there now, at this age, but I'm glad I experienced it back then.

People aren't allowed to touch paintings in museums for the same consequence I've endured. The oils from fingerprints steal some time from us, a little bit of life gone. My paint is nowhere near the quality used on museum paintings, so it's even more finicky. It's of lesser quality and breaks down faster. My lower quality means I'm something of a ticking clock until I dissolve completely, which might lend itself to people acting more carelessly around me. That's not a good reason, of course, and it's offensive, but that's how it goes. I care more about the hygiene of their touching than my broken-down colors, but I feel like that's reason enough. I don't deserve to be dirty, and human fingers are nasty. I don't know where those things have been.

I moved into that living room by way of a yard sale. When they were much younger, the Living Room People bought me from an older woman for a couple of dollars.

Far less than I'm worth. I don't remember anything about belonging to the older woman, but the entire sale was an insult. I don't forgive her, not necessarily, but I'm not dwelling on it because, again, there's nothing I can do. That sale was my upgrade; the Living Room People may have gotten me for cheap, but they showed me nothing but respect the entire time I hung. Actually, I don't remember my life much before them. In a lot of ways, hanging in their living room was when my life began.

Decades later, the Living Room People became Madison's parents. So, by association, I've known her for quite a long time. Madison was a tiny baby when I first met her, and all the way to now, she's grown up. I hung high in her parents' living room for those years while she grew, so I watched it all happen. Really, I saw enough to be thankful I wasn't hung in her bedroom. If I was in there, I think I'd be in much worse shape than just my current color fade. She was wild—I saw it and I heard it. I watched her from my spot high on the wall, all the while thankful for the immunity my height gave me. At least in those early years.

I remember a particular Christmas on the wall, watching kid Madison and her parents from above. I watched as she opened wrapped presents with a scowl on her face, tromping over the bits unwrapped just seconds earlier, and just about murdering everything in her wake. She plodded and howled around that room like she was battery-powered. I remember thinking she was uncontrolled, a brat, and thanking God for her inability to reach my face.

Madison got older, of course, and she slowed down. I saw that too. Her parents moved me from the living room wall to a new spot above an old-fashioned bed in what I think was the guest bedroom. I paid attention when they moved me, and so did she. In my new room, Madison came to visit me every day or so. Through those visits, I saw she didn't only slow down as she got older, but she also matured. Maybe she grew some appreciation for my beauty, too. Either that or I gained some sentiment.

Madison visited me in my new room every day or so, looked at me for a few minutes, moved me an inch to one side, then left again. That was our routine for years. I became fond of her through those visits. I got to watch her grow up and over the hill of her recklessness, first as a heavy-hearted teenager, then into a young adult. I grew protective of her because I saw how special she was. She was always sensitive, but even more so as she grew up and started coming into herself. Hanging as a painting in that house was like being an older sibling, but one she got along with.

Then one day, she stopped coming. A week went by—a week of silence that nearly killed me, if only I was alive. I listened closely for her voice in other rooms of the house, but she wasn't there. I hung and waited for the sounds of her mouth breathing or her feet slapping, but they never came. At the end of that week, I heard someone say she moved out and something about "mad," and I put the pieces together.

There was my answer: Madison moved to her own house. Without me. They didn't say that last part ("without you, Oscar"), but that's the part that hurt the most.

I was shocked, lonely, and nearly miserable about it. Those feelings mostly took me by surprise because I didn't expect to care as much as I did. It took her moving away for me to realize how fond I'd become of her and how I'd taken her company for granted. I was bound to her more than I realized, and she had to move out for me to appreciate her.

I must have shown my sadness with dulled colors or something because the Living Room People took me off the wall to throw me away. Or so I thought. Where they could have pitched me, though, they wrapped me in see-through pillow-like plastic, loaded me into a car, and took me away. They took me to visit my girl. We were reunited, and it felt good.

The Living Room People gave me to Madison as a housewarming present, I guess, because they carried me in to see her, then they left without me. I was over the moon about it, but not literally. I was over a table in the dining room of her new house. I was home.

When Madison's parents first pulled me from the plastic pillows, Madison stared at me for a few seconds, and a tear rolled down her cheek. Our reunion was much gloomier than I expected. I was immediately embarrassed, sad, and heartbroken that she could be so unhappy to see me. It felt like my emotions were sitting in the front row of a roller coaster: first climbing up, then speeding downhill a second later. Her tears, so genuinely wounded, reminded me of what I saw that Christmas in the living room. My insecurities shouted at me that I wasn't *good enough,* and she was acting like a *brat*. I'm not proud of that impulse.

Her tears ended differently than they did on that Christmas morning, though, because I could see a smile underneath. She hugged her parents, and I understood they were *happy* tears, and she wasn't upset to see me—she was overwhelmed, in a good way. I've never felt better and more relieved than at that moment. Madison thanked her parents as a smile spread across her face. She grabbed me by my top edges and carried me to a room with empty walls. The dining room, I know now. She held me in her arms as we spun around a few times, then she hung me in an empty space overlooking a table. Madison loved me still, and I was perfectly content. I *am* content.

She sometimes visits me in the dining room, but it's not nearly as often as when she was a kid. That's something I had to get used to all over again: my seclusion and being okay on my own. From my spot in the dining room, I can hear what's happening in the rooms around me, but I don't necessarily have to be a part of anything. It's cool, and I like that I can hear all the fuss, but sometimes I think I wouldn't mind being back in the middle. Now that she's older. Not as wild.

I'm thankful I get to see her at all though, honestly. When I first got to this place, she sometimes came to my room to light a candle and eat a meal by herself. Other times, she came with a boy. The same boy who lives here with her. I was thrilled, truly. I was happy to see her with someone who seemed to love her as much as I do. They looked good together, and it was good to see her happy. I haven't seen the two of them in a while, but they're probably just busy. I hear it. This new home isn't big like the Living Room people's, so I hear just about everything.

I hear when Madison is in her bedroom getting ready in the morning, when she's on the phone with her mother, when she's using the toilet, and when she's playing on her phone on the couch. When the boy is over, I hear them fight, and I hear them make up. People think I don't understand what's going on because I'm a painting, but I'm taking it all in. I take sides in their arguments, I have opinions on the clothes she wears, and I smell the food she burns in the kitchen. I just hang here, taking it in. These days, I'm more like her roommate. But one who can't talk back.

I've been hanging in Madison's dining room for a couple months now, and I'm starting to see her less and less. I hear her singing and I smell her attempts in the kitchen, but I haven't seen her wide smile or her pretty face in a while. I miss when we used to hang out more, but more than that, I hope she's happy.

The times she has come around to see me, she's alone and it's quick: to move me an inch to one side, push a vacuum around, or put away a dish. I appreciate her touch, as creepy as that sounds, but I understand there are more important things than me. A painting. I get that she can't spend as much time as she used to. She's busy now. I get it. It does get uncomfortable when I'm hanging crooked, though, even just a little bit. It throws my perspective way off. I guess it still bothers her on some level, too, because she has always been good about coming to straighten me out—even with everything she has going on. That's the lucky part I have in this. She's wise to that stuff.

She might also come in here because she wants to be with me, but I can't ever know. Maybe it's a little of both. At this point, I've been around for long enough to be her nostalgia, so it could very well be the latter. We're a team, me and her. Girl and painting.

Already told, I don't see her as much, but I hear her voice around me all the time. I think I could recognize it in a crowd of 1,000 people if I had to. In the few times I've seen her recently, she has popped her head or body in and out, stared at the walls, and spun in circles. It has been nice, I admit, that time together. Earlier today, she came in and hammered nails into the wall directly across. I don't know what she's up to, but I hope she'll hang something for me to look at. Some company. It gets quiet.

BANG.

I hear her familiar grunt, then her footsteps coming toward me.

"Here we go," Madison pounds into my room and says maybe to herself, but also maybe to me. She's holding a long box that reaches down to her toes. I watch, silently of course, as she slips the flap off the box's top and pulls out a gold frame with a piece of shiny, reflective glass in the center. I can only see a corner as it comes from the box, but just that much makes me nervous. When I look at it—into it—I see her face reflected in the glass. That part is nice. Her chin has that same smile spread across, so that makes me feel a little better. I'm just going to trust her on this one. Also, I don't have much choice.

Madison lifts the frame to the wall directly across from me, smiles for another second, nods her head once—I see it in the reflection—then walks out. She walks out and leaves me alone with the fancy, gold-framed piece. It's hanging directly across from me, so I can see my surroundings reflected back. I also see a reflection of myself for the first time since I was made so many years ago.

I wish I could take that part back. With every stroke on my body, I wish I could unsee it. I didn't like what I saw, not in the least.

The last time I saw myself was right after I was made. My artist held me in front of a mirror back then, presumably for me to admire his work, and that's the only memory I have. My colors were still vibrant, and my lines were crisp with contrast. He looked so proud of me, and I loved how that felt. I looked good.

Now, looking at myself in the reflection all this time later, I see the effect the years have had. I haven't aged well. My red is still red and my green is still green, but muted. There are chips in my frame from moving from house to house, and I'm covered in oil from years of fingerprints. My lines don't look crisp anymore. It's sad, and I wish I could take it back. I wish there was a way to unsee it.

I can't hide away with my insecurity like others can because I'm nailed to this wall, and the glass across from me is just as stuck as I am. I'm forced to stare at my insecurities day in and day out. My only option is to hang and look at me, staring back at me. I'm ever on hold and ever waiting for her to come back in to push the vacuum, put away a dish, and push me to one side. If I'm lucky, maybe she'll stand in front of me and block the view for a second. I'm trying to remember what I looked like that first day I was made so I can go back and dwell on just that.

One *long* second at a time, I'm trying to forget what I look like. All over again.

Sunday, October 27

I moved out of my parents' house and into an apartment almost three months ago, and I love it. I love it because it's *mine*. I don't have to share with anyone anymore. I'm still kind of adjusting to the solitude of it all, but there are some perks: I can play podcasts at full volume with music to sing along to; I can eat two handfuls of popcorn for dinner and not be accountable, and I can maintain a gremlin-looking face for the entire weekend with no one to judge. There's no challenge about my trips to the grocery store where I only come home with potato chips and grapes, when I meet up with friends at any hour of the night, or (just to show you I have range) when I don't leave my room for two straight days.

On the other hand, though, there's no one telling me to turn down my music, to eat more protein, or to keep a more normal schedule. I'm alone, a full-blown adult, and I don't like it. Freedom is great, and it might sound like I'm on top of the world, but I actually don't prefer solitude. I've never lived alone before, not even close, and I miss a lot about the commotion. I've always had it; I lived with my parents until I left for college, then with two roommates during all four years on campus, and then back with my parents for two years after graduation. Now that I'm trying to be that full-blown adult, though, I live full-blown by myself. I'm used to and okay with the loneliness of not having a romantic partner, but I've never actually been *alone*.

So, after I graduated, I took my time moving out of my parents' house. It took me two years, actually, before I finally did: I got a from-home job that didn't require much of me, and I signed a lease for that home. An apartment in the city, all by myself. In a way, I guess I wanted to prove to myself that I could do it. I *can* do it. In another way, it was a giant act of self-sabotage.

I applied for and got the from-home job shortly before I moved from my parents' house, my intentions being to give me more time to spend in my lovely, quiet apartment. I thought I would want that. I thought I would love the isolation of the day, every workday spent in my own cave. I thought I'd only have to be alone until 5 p.m., which is when Charlie got off work and came over for dinner, and that my aloneness would have an endpoint. I thought I was giving myself room to be alone, but avoiding ever having to feel *alone*.

In the case of Charlie's reliable 5 p.m. companionship, from-home work sounded like a bright idea. In practice, though, when Charlie and I aren't amatory and when he doesn't come to me at dinnertime, I'm alone all day. *All day.*

Another point about working from home is I don't have an obligation to leave my house if I don't want to. Now that I'm single I rarely have an obligation, so I rarely leave. It works. Actually, it's cool because I don't have to put up much effort into how I look-I don't have coworkers, and Charlie and I have gotten *comfortable*-but the downside is I've had trouble making friends. You can imagine. How are adults supposed to meet people if not at work?

At the gym? *I don't go.*

At church? *I need to find one.*

Through mutual friends? *I need friends before I can be friends with their friends.*

I didn't like the solitude at first, and I had trouble with the fact that my apartment is completely silent until I make the noise. *Does that make sense?* I've never been a noise-driven person, not particularly, but I do like having commotion around me. That's the first thing that stood in my face when I moved out: I spend most of my time alone now, and I have to be okay with that. I considered getting a cat for company, but I'm not trying to clean a litter box.

Having Charlie around helps some, but nothing about our relationship is consistent. We were on good terms when I was moving in, so he helped move boxes and get me settled. We played the roles of "domesticated" for a week or so: cooking alongside each other, eating dinners by candlelight in the dining room, and sharing a tube of toothpaste. Living like that felt normal and like something I could get used to. Then, of course, we slipped back into another "rough patch," and he hasn't been around lately. But it's okay. I'm trying to be okay with being on my own.

A fun part of this apartment is I get to decorate it in my own style. It's just a bunch of little things because I don't have much money to spend yet, but I'm figuring out what my style looks like. It's fun and, turns out, it's contrary to my parents'. That means I'm filling this space with all things new, with one exception: a painting of a red barn in a field that hung in their house for as long as I can remember. They brought it to me as a house-warming gift a few weeks after I moved in, and I actually cried when I saw it. *Happy* tears. Charlie made fun of it when he came over that same evening, but he also didn't understand its nostalgia. I hadn't let him into the loneliness that swallows me when he isn't there, when the apartment is quiet, or how the silence can feel like every bone in my body is screaming at me for a distraction. Charlie doesn't know any of that, and I used his ignorance to justify myself out of being annoyed with him about his teasing. Only in hindsight do I see how rude he can be. He doesn't even try to understand.

The farm scene doesn't really match the style of the rest of my apartment, so I gave it its own space in my tiny, apartment-sized dining room. That painting has a lot of sentimental value, even though it's kind of old and ugly. I think my parents got it at a yard sale when they first got married, some thirty years ago, and they hung it in their house-my old house-for as long as I can remember. I went to that farm painting again and again when I was a kid, so it comes with a lot of memories. Mostly good ones.

This part is cheesy: as a kid, I think I found comfort in the fact that no matter how cold the weather or how bad my day, the farm, field, and clouds were the same. Their colors weren't always bright-they've faded with time-but the painted sun is always shining. I looked after that painting just like it looked after me through the years: I blew the dust off when I grew tall enough to reach, I kept it company when Mom moved it to the guest room, and I made sure it hung straight on the wall. I didn't have a lot of friends back then, so I had plenty of extra effort to give.

I'm really happy to have the farm in my apartment now. I don't see it except when I go into my dining room to straighten up every day or so, but it's nice to have a bit of *home* in my new home. I'm proud of the space I've made for myself, even though it's not as bougie as the space at my parents'. I think I'm doing okay here. So far.

My solitude has gone through stages, but I guess it had to. When I first moved in, I avoided silence like it was an annoying boy at recess. When Charlie and I are good, *alone* is an easy thing to avoid; he stays over so much that he basically lives in the apartment with me. For the first weeks I lived here, I was spoiled by him being around all the time. I didn't realize how much I hate the silence, though, until we had an argument and he left. But he left, and I'm *alone.* I have to be okay with that. I don't need a *boy* to be happy, especially one as volatile as Charlie. I know how to be alone, and I can do this.

In the absence of another person-my parents or my boyfriend-I'm trying to make my apartment less shallow. I don't want my place to feel how my aloneness feels, so I'm making an effort: I bought two mirrors, three succulents, and a tiny golden frog with a crown on its head. Mirrors because they make the rooms look bigger and full of people. *Full of people,* in this case, means me over and over again. I realize that. It's still better than nothing.

The frog was on the sale counter, and it's fine. I'm still finding my style.

I got succulents because I like plants, but I forget to water them-succulents will stand more of a chance. Now you see why I don't want a cat? I've been down this road before.

"Here we go," I say to myself, or to the room. I pick up a box that held the first mirror. Talking aloud and narrating helps with the silence, so I've made that something of a habit. People talk to themselves all the time. I'm not the crazy one. Or if I am, I don't care.

One of the mirrors is big and long, and the other is wide and fat. Both have gold frames because gold feels *sophisticated*. I read on some home design website that "mirrors are good to make tiny, apartment-sized rooms feel like comfortable, spacious suites." So, thank you, internet; I'm using the mirrors' reflections to trick myself into feeling less alone. That second reason is just my hope, and it'll be a miracle if it works.

Starting in my dining room, I hang the mirror's gold frame on the wall opposite my red barn. It looks good there, and the room feels a tiny bit bigger. I smile big into the mirror, and there's that instant relief. Whether the relief is from my own decoration or from standing next to an image of myself, it doesn't matter. I'm all about the illusions here.

Living on my own has more pros than cons, and the few cons disappear when Charlie and I are good. The solitude that comes with not sharing my space is something I'll have to get used to, I guess, but I think I'll end up liking it. Living alone after our breakup has been good for my openly crying and moping, but probably not as much for my mental health. I don't know. Maybe I'll get a cat.

Wednesday, October 30

I've never had my heart broken-shattered-before, so I've had a lot to learn. This is the first time I've really had to test my strength in an impossible situation, and that's how my grief over losing Charlie feels: *impossible.*

The pain is tangible. I can taste it-it's sour, like a mouthful of grapefruit. Sometimes it feels like a knife is twisting in my stomach and scraping across my lining. My pain is so intense, it can feel like maybe I won't make it to the other side of my sadness. It's like I don't know what to *do* with myself. How do people go through this more than once in their lives? And how can *anything* be worth this? It's wearing me down. I feel like I've already fallen apart.

Maybe I'm overdramatic, but these feelings are all new to me. Remember, I just bought that bathing suit.

I'm still raw. Someday, I might get a taste for that grapefruit, and I might even grow thankful for the lessons I'm learning through this struggle. But right now it just sucks.

Living alone has introduced me to myself from a new perspective. At least now I can admit that I'm not *not* annoying. Charlie used to call me *too much*, and I can't stop thinking about that. Maybe he had a point? All this time in my reflection is making me second-guess what I thought was true and what I thought was just Charlie's cruel words. Maybe he was right about everything he said. I don't know, but my doubt might be my answer. Charlie isn't a very patient person, but I'm not sure if that's just how he is, or how he is with me. I have reasons behind what he called my *madness*, but he didn't even try to understand.

I've thought a lot about this, about him, and that's what I've landed on: he doesn't care enough. Maybe knowing that will help my heart heal from him. Or maybe not.

The things Charlie defines as my *madness* feel like my common sense, and maybe a bit of his immaturity. He lives in a house with two other guys, frat-house-style, so a lot of his cruelty comes from a place of not empathizing. He's in that house with two roommates who let everyday tasks either fall to collaboration or just not get done. A house full of dudes won't care as much about lights left on, dried toothpaste in the sink, blankets spread lazily on the couch, or breadcrumbs next to the toaster.

I don't care about the breadcrumbs either, but you see my point; they *definitely* don't care. A lot of my madness started when I signed the lease and started paying the bill for this place. My parents paid the utility bills when I lived with them, so most of the consequences went over my head. I would leave the lights on, the water running, and the refrigerator door wide open without a second thought. That brand of carelessness is wasteful, and it all costs something. I see that now. On my own, I don't turn the lights on unless I'm in the room; I don't leave the water running while I brush my teeth, and I close the dang refrigerator door. I'm not *mad*-I'm responsible. And now that I'm the breadwinner, I'm trying to be mindful.

Some things I do take a little too far, I'll give him that. But everyone has something in that category, don't they? I turn off the lights when I leave the room, okay, but that's not my end. I rarely turn them on during the day, and when

I need them at night, I use them sparingly. I turn them on when I go to the bathroom, then turn them off to wash my hands. I know where the soap is and I can feel for a towel, so what's the need? I shower in the dark most of the time, except after those late nights with friends. I rarely turn on the lights when I eat alone because lighting a candle doesn't cost me anything and, ya know, it sets a mood. The mood is of romance and of conservation. Romance *with* myself and conservation *for* myself.

I live alone, and *none of this is hurting anyone*. It's not a big deal.

It is to Charlie, though. He has a hard time with some of the ways I do things. He doesn't understand but, remember, he doesn't try too. He gets hung up on the question of *why* I do some of the things I do, like *why* I spend "so much time in the dark" and *why* I care "so much" about how my "junky-looking pillows are thrown on the couch." Those pillows were the first pieces of decoration after I moved out on my own, so that one hurt.

I don't expect him to understand any of it any more than I don't have an answer to any of his questions. And that was frustrating for us both. The difference between Charlie and me is that I'm stuck with my rituals. He's not. He can just walk away and leave them and me behind. And that's exactly what he does.

He leaves, and that's why we're stuck on a stream, of sorts: off, on, and off again. I think he knows he has other people he can run to, so he keeps a short fuse for how much of me he'll put up with. More or less, I'm a convenience.

When we're good, we're happy, and he's around. When we're not, though-he's *gone*. Like now. His leaving puts me in my place and, you know this, it doesn't feel good.

But Charlie is all I have. Starting over with someone new-assuming I can find someone new-would mean starting at the beginning. In that way, I guess he's also my convenience.

You can imagine, this is not a stream I'd prefer to float on. But Charlie feels like the best I'll ever have, so I put up with it. Everyone has *things*-he has plenty of his own-but the tricky part of relationships is finding someone who will put up with them. For the most part, Charlie and I put up with each other's, and that feels like something. Charlie's *thing* is his inconsistency, and I'm figuring out a way to work around it. For as long as I can, anyway.

Monday, November 11

"Madison," Mom sighs in relief and immediately launches in, "How are you, sweetie?" The clock beside me reads 2:30 p.m., but I'll never tell her she woke me from a nap.

"Hey, Mom," I say with my voice a few octaves higher than normal. It's the first time I've spoken all day, and I think using a higher pitch will hide the *sad* in my voice. I haven't left my apartment for two days; I'm taking a nap in the middle of work, and I'm still wearing the same t-shirt with the holes and over-stretched neckline from a day ago.

Somehow, I feel like talking with my normal voice will give away all my secrets.

"I'm all right. I took a long lunch break today."

The truth is, I haven't actually accomplished anything outside some light furniture rearranging and browsing the internet. My workstation is three long strides from my kitchen, so there's not much to stop me from eating snacks throughout my entire day. So I do. Of course I do. My life feels like the beginning of a movie-the scenes before the sloppy, lazy, and possibly overweight main character has an epiphany and turns their life around. I'm not fat and I don't need an enormous plot twist to snap me out of this, but you know what I mean. I'm just alone, and I'm sad.

"What have you been doing?" she asks. We usually catch up with each other every day or so, but we haven't for three days, a week? I've lost track. The days I spend in my quiet, darkened apartment run together.

"I've been busy," I say. A half lie. "There's so much to do. Living here is more fun than I thought, though." A full lie.

The busyness comes from trying to keep out of my apartment as much as I can during the day. I stay busy to distract myself from my loneliness and because I think about Charlie when it's quiet. I also think about him first thing in the morning and at the last part of the night. So I actively try to keep myself away from those times: I go for morning runs, I talk to myself in the silence, and I stay out late with whomever I can rally. I put effort into how I look for my own confidence, and so people will like me. How I look and how I'm healing mentally is my hobby these days. I just want to fit in and prove that I'm okay with being single. *I'm okay.*

If I'm honest, though, I'm miserable. I'm trying so hard to not let my heartache swallow me, but I'm tired. I'm scared to sit still or be quiet for too long because I don't know if I'll be able to get back up. It's embarrassing how disabled and powerless I feel, and even worse when I think that he's impervious to all of it. Charlie has knocked me so far off course, and it's embarrassing. I feel pathetic, and I don't know how to fix it.

"I'm decorating a little bit," I say, changing the subject. "I haven't bought much new stuff, but I've rearranged since you were here."

The things I don't say: it's a distraction. When I start to get in my head about him, I slide the couch to another spot. I start thinking about a good time with Charlie, and I move the TV to the other side of the room. I wonder what he's doing at that moment, and I flip the rug to the opposite wall. Nothing has stayed in its place for more than a day since I moved in.

"Have you unpacked all the boxes yet?"

"I'm getting close," I say. "There are still some in the back room, but they're almost empty."

A lesson I'm learning during this tandem breakup and move is that I can be messy about some things-my apartment, for now-but meticulous about others. I choose my battles, I guess, but there's no pattern to which battles I'll choose. My process of adjustment to my new, adult-like lifestyle would drive some people crazy. Charlie, I guess, is one of those people.

Crumbs on the countertop can cover the entire surface area, and I won't notice them until someone points them out. But if the milk is a half-hour past expiration or if my gums aren't practically bleeding after brushing my teeth, it makes me so anxious that I can't move past it. If the pillows on my couch aren't equal in number on either side, I'll drop whatever's in my hands to switch them over. But if there's a box in the middle of the living room or you've tracked mud in from the front door? It might stay there a week, and I won't think twice.

I've gotten a little better about some things-the bleeding gums, for example-but only just. I choose which battles I'll fight, but I don't actually consciously get a choice. It's like there's a miniature Madison in my subconscious, directing the orchestra of my anxiety. She sounds cute, except she's a loose cannon who has way too much power over my every day.

"Do you want to meet for lunch this week?" Mom asks after a longer pause. I can tell she's seeing through my mask of a high voice and forced enthusiasm because our conversation is strained. Awkward, almost. I tried to hide it from her, at least, but it was a long shot.

"That would be nice," I say, relaxing back into my normal pitch. There's no point in pretending to be okay when I'm not. I'm not okay at all. I just don't want her to worry about me. "Thursday would work. I'll take another long lunch."

"See you on Thursday," she says with a smile I can hear through the phone.

"See ya Thursday," I say.

Paul

I'm turned On by a few different people, but a girl named Madison really gets me heated. She turns me On the most and the easiest. I spend most of my time turned Off, but I never have to be for long; Madison turns me On a lot—most times I see her. She doesn't turn me On as much as she used to, but I spend a good amount of time that way.

I prefer when I'm turned On, but I guess that's no surprise. You understand: when I'm On, my whole body gets warm, it starts humming, and an energy runs through me that I don't know how to explain. In a good way. That euphoria never lasts long, though; when I'm On, I always get turned right back Off. I like everything about how I feel when I'm On, but I understand why I can't stay like that all the time. I get it.

My name is Paul. I'm screwed tight over a mirror that's set behind a sink in her bathroom. It feels like the Command

Center in here, like I'm in the perfect position to be in the center of everything. She turns me On for quick spurts in the mornings while she gets ready, at midday with varying levels of mania, and in the evenings when she's more undone. I'm here for it all, and I can adapt to her: spotlight when she's happy and lowlight when she's sad. She has been sad here a lot lately, but that has happened before. She'll bounce out of it—she always does—and I'll be with her for it all. I'm not going anywhere, even if I could.

Working as a lightbulb in this bathroom is kind of like riding a carousel of her every day. I'm on a track of up, down, On, Off, back up, and back down. Not everyone could handle that, I don't think, but I'm used to the constant swing. I've *grown* used to it.

I spend my days flipping from On to Off and, maybe surprisingly, I don't know which position I like better. They're both good for different reasons:

I'm hyper-aware of all the activity and feelings around me when I'm On. I'm providing light to her, either spot or low, and it feels good. I feel good.

Then when I switch Off, it's dark, and that's a nice contrast. Being Off is a break from my work, which is important because I have to cool down every once in a while. It's hard to manage all that heat in my belly without a recess.

A lot more goes into being a lightbulb than you think.

She's usually with me when I'm turned On, so there are always other things going on around me at the same time as the commotion inside me. That activity makes it hard to focus on and enjoy myself turned On, as you can imagine.

It's all kind of weird timing. But that's how it has always been. I'm well used to the challenge, but it's a lot. It's just a lot.

There used to be more action in this bathroom, and my job used to be way more exciting. Well, it wasn't that there was *more* action, as much as it was a *different kind* of action. A boy used to clomp around here every day or so, and she would hang around more: in front of the mirror, standing in the shower, and sitting on the toilet. When she was with me so much, those were the exciting parts. I was on spot a lot back then.

Then things changed, suddenly, and I've had to switch back to low. The boy doesn't come through anymore; I spend more time in the Off, and, when she does come in, she's not as buoyant. I've been around for long enough to know the difference. There might be some connection between that boy and her apathy, but I can't be sure. Whatever bad it is, though, I've had to adapt.

I'm thankful for the time I spend in the Off position, even if it's more often than not lately. Having a variance between the two means I have something to look forward to: either the stimulation of On or the peaceful untethered-ness of Off. There's a time and place for all that stimulus, but all at once, all the time, ain't it. Being turned On feels good and it's fun, but Off is my rest.

There's not much else to say about when I'm in darkness because there's not much to it. It's just very dark and basically quiet. I spend the time cooling down from being On which, as I said, is crucial. Off is quiet and peaceful, except for the echo of activity in other rooms. But it's just as easy to tune those out. When I'm Off, it feels like the world stops. Or, at least, slows to crawl.

In a way, I guess, my world does stop. But in a good and necessary way. I need that darkness, that break, to get ready for my next round of stimulation. I always have to be ready for when she turns me On again.

There's a thing called *Burnout*, and I've heard enough about it to feel it's looming over me. Actually, it's the only reason the word "anxiety" is in my vocabulary. Being turned On is great and I love the work I do, but bad things are coming for me.

Okay, *one* bad thing.

I guess everyone is afraid of dying on some level, but my death just feels more dramatic. I envision my Burnout like a storm cloud hanging above my head, ready to open at any second. That's just to say that it's impending and proving impossible for me to ignore—perhaps because I'm left to hang here thinking about it all my days, save for the minutes I'm turned On. Burnout is the end for me, but, more technically, it means my twirly wire inside is somehow used up, worn out, and I'm dead. Kaput. There's no coming back.

For the most part, she's pretty good about my preservation and keeping that wire from burning too hot. We're a good, implicit match. As much as I like being On, she seems to know that keeping me Off makes the most sense—at least when there's another light or she's not in the room. It hasn't always been like that, though. There is, apparently, a learning curve. One time, long ago and before she got smart about it, she left me On for way too long. This memory still makes me feel awful. She only made that mistake once and hasn't done it since, though, because I think it traumatized us both. Thank goodness. No one likes to be turned On with no one else around, and that includes me. That was the first and last time.

I remember she was in a hurry the day it happened, but I never figured out why. In the disorder of it all, she ran in here, turned me On to stare in the mirror and paint her eyes with a tiny brush, then ran out as quickly as she came. She ran out before turning me Off, I'll repeat that part, and I wasn't allowed my peaceful cooling. I felt helpless, and I got angry. But my anger didn't do anything about the fact that I was forgotten. How I feel isn't important. I know that.

As a lightbulb, I don't have control over anything that happens to me, so all I can really do is watch the world happen. And get angry. A part of me was curious and a little excited to experience the extended arousal without all her extra distractions, but that was only a tiny part of me. I was curious about what it would feel like, but I was also nervous.

As it happened and I was hanging On for so long, my nerves gave me a hard time and I couldn't enjoy anything. I was so focused on my liquidation that I almost turned completely numb. I figured I'd either run out of juice and never see her again, or I'd catch fire and burn up. My body grew so hot that I started anticipating the latter. No matter how it happened, I thought her mistake would be my end. So both options sent me to panic. I almost completely missed out on the arousal of being turned On.

In the end, it was nothing like I expected. Where I thought I'd feel exhilarated and passionate, I was hot, very hot, and I was stressed out. It was dull compared to what I'm used to. There's nothing to go on in the bathroom when she's not there, so I just hung, heated up, and remained.

It felt like I waited for a day, maybe two, for her to come back for me. I tried not to count the passing time while I heated because that would only drag it out. So I can't really be sure how long I burned up there. When she did finally come to flip me Off, it had to have been only seconds before my body caught fire. I felt it: my body was blistering, and my hums were near deafening. She saved me, in a way, but I didn't appreciate her complete indifference when she saw I was left On. In fact, it infuriated me even more.

Remember, though, I'm a lightbulb, and there's nothing I can do toward revenge. "Feeling angry" is just about my biggest threat.

She flipped me Off and shut the bathroom door to my complete darkness—both in the room and in my belly. That part was nice, but I was still fuming, in all definitions of the word. Her recklessness wasted about eight hours of my life, which is a price we'll both pay when the Burnout comes eight hours earlier than she planned. Maybe then she'll learn her lesson.

Since that first mistake, she hasn't left me turned On. Her indifference told me she didn't care much either way—whether I was On or Off—but maybe I was unfair. She seems to care enough to not leave me burning alone again, at least, and that's mostly enough. I'm not turned On as much these days, not for as long as I used to be, and I'm usually only On at night. But there's something about the nighttime that makes being turned On better anyway, so I guess it's fine. I like being On and I regret not being able to arouse it in myself, but I'm thankful for her company when I am. That time when I was On with no one around was wholly unsatisfying, and I don't want to do that again.

I know the Burnout will happen someday, and I'm still not sure how I feel about it. It doesn't much matter how I feel because I can't do anything to stop it, but I still want to figure out how I do. On one hand, Burnout just means I'll be permanently Off. *Retired.* And that wouldn't be the worst thing. It sounds peaceful, maybe a bit boring, but it's a break I often look forward to. I won't have to bother with a smokin' hot belly, but I think I'll lament not having anything to do or see in my darkness. I'd also miss her company, sort of. I'll cross all these bridges when I get to them, I guess. No point thinking about it now.

I don't have any stories or advice from the other bulbs that burned before me because I don't see them after they're done being screwed. That's okay because they're all probably exhausted from their work, and I have a lot of questions. There are just a lot of changes ahead. I'm at her mercy now, hanging around and anticipating the next time she's going to turn me On. At this point, I feel like a teenage boy.

I'm one of the lucky ones—I know that—because I get turned On every day by her hands. There's something about Madison that makes me warm, my body hum, and an electricity shoot through me that I can't put words to. She turns me On, and she seems to want me as much as I do her. When she turns me On, it's hot and often, and that feels rare. I don't think she has that kind of connection with any other bulbs, so that's enough to make me feel better. It's enough to hold me over, at least, until the next time I'm turned On.

Tuesday, November 19

Charlie called yesterday, and he wants to meet for coffee next week. To talk, I guess. Meeting him in public like that feels very formal, very adult, but I guess that's what we are: two adults in a relationship.

Are we in a relationship? *Sorta.*

Or, maybe he wants to meet up and tell me more reasons why we *can't* be in a relationship, why I'm *unstable*, or why I need *help.* There's only one way to find out: jump back into Charlie's deep end, headfirst, and with my eyes closed. I don't see another choice. I need to make some improvements first, though. Some effort.

I passed by a couple of "phases" while I was growing up: the makeup phase, the selfie phase, and the paying-more-than-ten-dollars-for-one-article-of-clothing phase. I breezed past them either out of my laziness, my self-confidence, or my budget. It was likely a combination of the three: I didn't make the effort because I didn't feel like I needed the help enough to spend the money for it. I justified myself into yoga pants and a ponytail almost every day of the week. It was great, and life was uncomplicated.

I'm playing a different game now, though, and this one is asking more of me. I agreed to meet Charlie for coffee, and my plan is for him to take one look at me and want me back. I want the ball back in my court, then I can decide if *I* want Charlie back in *my* life.

I do, but I'd still like to have the ball back.

I've never made much effort with how I look around him, and I think that's one of the things he likes about me. But the stakes are higher now, and nothing can be as casual as it used to be. Now I'm playing the Game, and I'm not even sure with whom or what I'm competing. I'm going to show up, though, and I'm going to get him back. I'm not entirely sure how I'll do it, but I am confident I'll be sitting in the driver's seat this time.

My confidence must count for something, right?

Makeup is my first move because it feels like it should be. I also thought it would be a cheaper, more user-friendly place to start. I'm laughing at myself now, though. I'm the *most* naive, and no sooner than I walked into the makeup store, I was fighting against turning right back around and walking out. There's nothing cheap about that stuff and nothing that doesn't almost intimidate the nerve out of me. I want Charlie back more than I wanted out of there, though, so I picked out two what-felt-like-beginner's items to get me started.

I've worn mascara before, but that was long ago and only a couple of times. Still, it's a somewhat-familiar comfort. One of Charlie's *things*-a different kind of *thing*-is a girl's eyes, so there's a big piece of my justification. I felt justified in paying triple the amount I expected mascara to cost, and again when I picked a set of fake lashes. Just in case. Mine are a bit lacking these days, so the fakes are for backup. I'm okay with showing up as the same ol' *bare-faced Madison*, but the least I can do is be a *bare-faced Madison with beautiful eyes*.

Baby steps.

In my imagination, I have long, full, dark eyelashes like when I was a teenager. But I don't think I'll ever get back there. At least not anytime soon. That's not me being pessimistic, either, just practical. My eyelashes fall out a lot, or they come loose and I have to remove them. Gravity doesn't (or I don't) give mine the chance to hang for long, so I pick out some fakes for backup.

I thought all girls shared my lash, lack of lash, problem. I don't know-I skipped over this phase. But recently, I've started to think there's something about me that makes my lashes come loose more than other people's. Maybe? I pull at them sometimes, but I've done that forever, even when they used to be full. Most of the time, I pull because the lash has already come loose, and I'm trying to keep it from dropping on my face or into my eye. Everyone does that, but maybe I do it with more delight. I mostly just sweep, though, and I hardly ever pull.

I've tried using tweezers to remove a *few* lashes a *couple of* times, but it was too intense for me. I read about it on the internet once, how people tweeze "to prevent eye injury" with their sweep, so I just wanted to try. The tweezers made the pull from my lid more accurate, I guess, but it stung too sharply. Too intense. I just use my fingers now.

I guess I do have a *thing* about my body hair; I don't like it. I wish I could wave a wand to take out all the hair on my body, but I'm a reasonable person, and I deal with my hair in reasonable ways: I shave my armpits every couple of days, I keep my leg hair at a bare minimum, and I pluck the rare eyebrows that grow in the middle. It's not anything special. Sometimes, I yank at my eyelashes, but you won't find someone who doesn't. I shave, pluck, and trim all the hair I'm socially "allowed to," but if I had my way, I'd disappear it all. My pulling and *sweeping*-that's what we're calling it-of my eyelashes are things about me that irritate Charlie, so they're the things I keep to myself.

That's not my keeping a secret as much as an omission. I omit some small stuff to save myself from hearing about how *irrational* and *stupid* I can be. I've accepted that he'll never understand some things about me, and I'm okay with that. I just don't feel like hearing about it.

I'm *sad*, and I'm sick of being sad. I'm at least admitting to that now, so there's the first step. I was able to ignore my sadness for a long time with my schoolwork, the commotion of living with my parents, then moving into my own space, but it has caught up to me. I thought my independence would somehow override my sadness but, in a way, it only cast a spotlight. The makeup, the constant awareness of what I look like, and the eggshells I've been walking on around Charlie are exhausting. If all this works and I get Charlie back, though, I call it my small price to pay. The upgrades I'm making to myself are just part of playing the Game.

I'll say this again and until it checks out: I'll do what it takes. Even if that means I have to go back to the makeup store, take an extra fifteen minutes getting ready in the morning, or spend my entire paycheck upgrading my image and wardrobe, I'll do what it takes. Maybe in the process of getting Charlie back, I might also get back some pieces of myself.

Carol

I've already been hanging for longer than I thought I'd be, so I can't imagine I'll be around for much more. Based on what I've seen, I'll likely drop out or be pulled out before I'm ready and before my job is done. I wish I had more doubt about that. More hope.

My name is Carol, and I'm working as a guardian, of sorts, for the most important part of her body: the eyeball. I'm rooted beside—crammed against—her ball, and I'm meant to block dirt and muck from getting stuck. It's an amazingly never-ending responsibility. It's a fun one for me though, kind of.

Like I said, I won't be around for long. So I'm working hard while I still can. While I'm still around. My "working hard" looks like flapping around a lot, and fast, and that's not too far from my normal. I do get seconds of stillness sometimes, but they're nothing to count on; for the most part, I'm always moving. Even while she sleeps,

I move around—less often and it's a little different, but my job doesn't just stop. It's exhausting. But this is what I signed up for.

It's amazing how much junk from the world tries to get past me and into her eyeball. The job gets harder every day—every minute—because our numbers are in steady decline. The lashes around me are constantly falling out or being pulled out, so I can't really count on anyone. I'm working hard and moving as fast as I can, but this job is no joke. And it's only getting worse. I would like to be annoyed with the others for not hanging out to help for longer than they do, but they don't control when they come and go, so I can't even blame them for leaving. But that doesn't make it any less inhibiting. And I guess they feel the same way about me too. Still, it's hard not to get annoyed when I see one of them floating away in the breeze while I'm giving my all to this job.

I guess I'm more annoyed at my situation than with the other lashes. But that's only my hindsight talking.

I'm surrounded by lashes on both sides and the lid below, but it still gets lonely. Our sudden and unexpected dropout is why no one really makes friends with each other up here—we don't know how long the friendship will last before we have to jump ship. A bit of loneliness is better than the certain heartbreak of losing a friend, though, so I'm fine with it. Because I have to be.

Her pulling—I call it "ripping"—us out is very unpleasant. I see it happen all the time. That's one thing I actually *can* count on: it will be my doom. Some lashes, who've been around longer than me, say she used to use thin metal teeth to rip us out, and it was a vicious kind of torture. She only uses her fingers to rip us these days, but those are just as horrifying.

I grew in near the end of the Metal Tooth Era, but I was around to say goodbye to the last lash that left by way of those teeth. Bryson. He was rooted two lashes down from me. He left when I was still young and had only just arrived, but I'll never forget the sound he made while he was being ripped out. Every rip since him has been with her fingers but, still, he taught me a lesson about learning names: don't do it. It's not worth it. I was young back then, and I still had a lot of spirit left. It didn't take long for me to grow hard to all of this, though.

But not *literally* hard. Not yet. We'll get to that.

These days, she rips us with two of her fingers: the longest and the fattest. The double-edged sword of living alongside the eyeball is that I see everything coming, including those two. Those fingers could mean she's just going to rub us back and forth—uncomfortable, but no comparison—or she's going to rip us out and drop us in the wind. The unknown. If the latter, I can only hope I'm not the unlucky lash she chooses. I can't do anything to influence her choice, though, so call me helpless. I've even seen her take two of us at a time, but she usually just picks one. We don't know if it's a One Day or a Two Day until it's over, and we're still hanging. A lot of my existence is in the gray area.

At the beginning of my time on the lid, there was a lash named Martha. Even though she was below me and far to the left, her loud and self-important voice was perfectly clear. After every Rip, she would boast about not being chosen and how she "deserves to hang longer." Whatever that means. Not many of us liked her.

One day, as if it was planned, Martha started a sentence ("I knew she wouldn't pick me because I'm f—") and, before she could finish, she was ripped from her root. Martha was outta there. That was one of the only times that we, the remaining lashes, made a noise—a celebratory one—at the same time. Martha was a mess, and I don't regret learning her name.

Even with the sharp end of fate's sword staring back at me, I still feel better off than her head or nose hairs. I wouldn't trade my ability to see things. I prefer my spot above her eyeball because there are no surprises, but I'm still not over the moon. The view is nice, but it can be my nightmare just as easily as my daydream. It's my advantage or my handicap, but at least my handicap isn't a blind one. I see all things, so I feel like I live life more fully than the other hairs on her body.

I've seen the way she decorates her apartment, how she's dressed when she looks in the mirror before going out, and I've seen the boy she's spending so much time with. I know that she writes in a notebook, and I get to read her words. She spends a good amount of her time in the darkness, so I see a lot in the shadows, but she does light a candle while she writes. Thank goodness for that because squinting is a whole different challenge.

The stuff she writes in her journal is mostly junk about a boy called Charlie and how they're getting along. Sometimes she writes things about her routines, too, and those things are worthwhile. But mostly it's boring. But it doesn't take a lot to keep me interested, hanging up here all day, so I read it all. Recently, she has written a lot about sadness, frustration, and confusion with Charlie. There's my tiny bit of justification for all her crying recently. All the tears I've had to deal with.

Really, I don't have room to complain as much as the others.

Her ripping is random, as far as I can tell, so I'm just thankful I haven't been chosen yet. When one of us is ripped, the eyeball fills with water for all of us left behind to work with. That excess water is a memorial service, of sorts, for the lost lash, and it's our clue to get to work: bat and flap until it's back under control. The more lashes we lose, though, the less help we have and the more difficult our job becomes. Especially recently, I've had to let a lot of water fall past.

My earliest and closest call to leaving this lid was from my neighbor. Ada. We grew in at the same time, and both of us made the mistake of becoming fond.

Ada was ripped young—we were both young. I remember watching that finger coming at me and thinking, "This is it. Here we go." I was so sure I'd been chosen, but then I didn't feel her fingers on my head, and I didn't feel myself tearing from the root. But Ada did—her screams left no doubt. I lost her that day, and I think that's when I finally learned the lesson about friendship. You already know the lesson (don't do it), but it took a couple of friends ripped out for me to adopt it. Eventually, I did, though. I'm a work in progress.

Ada left like a storm, and that's how I would like to go. When she was ripped, our eyeball entered a season of havoc. The space around the ball that's usually white turned pink, red veins grew like vines stretching from the outside in, and the eye filled, then refilled with water. That was more work for me, but I was working so hard that I didn't have time to be bitter.

While all that was going on, a crust grew around my waist. For some reason. And it was uncomfortable. It felt like how I imagined it would feel to wear a skirt of bread-crumbs—except these breadcrumbs were much tinier, and they were stuck. The girl shared my discomfort, I guess, because she rubbed us back and forth more than usual, and her eye kept filling with liquid. She started yanking at our tips more—which helped to get some crumbs off—but it was dangerous for us who were hanging on. The crumb-version of her yanking was more gentle, so it didn't rip many of us from our roots. That was the only good part.

In a way, we and the girl worked together to get those crumbs off. But we lashes took the biggest expense.

I'm proud to have lasted through that. I'm proud of us who made it through the redness and the crumbs, but it's hard not to lament the ones we lost—some good lashes were ripped before they were ready. But that's how this story goes. I didn't know their names, of course, but I knew the value they brought to the work.

She didn't tolerate the veins or the extra watering for long, thank goodness, so maybe we won't have to go over that trauma again. After about a day, she started dropping some kind of magic water into the ball. It sounds counterintuitive because of the extra work of extra water, but I was happy for this work. The magic healed her eyeball, and we were back to normal after one more night of those breadcrumbs around my waist. "Exhausting" took a new meaning.

After that ordeal, we're even more scarce now. I thought I was lonely before because I wasn't making friends with the other lashes, but now I'm lonely because I'm actually *almost alone*. I wish there were more of us, and I wish I didn't feel like the only one up here doing any work. More eyelashes would mean a lighter workload, okay, but it would also mean I'm not by myself.

I've seen what happens after we're ripped out, and that's where a lot of my anxiety comes from. This is a time when my view is my handicap; she doesn't rip us out and drop us, left to float away with the wind. To the contrary, I've seen her put us between her fingers and roll us around for what I'm guessing feels like a certain forever. One time, I saw her rip out a fellow eyelash, roll him in her fingers, then pop him into her mouth. It was repulsive. Horrifying. I'm not sure which is worse: being trapped in and rolled between those fingers for an indeterminate amount of time or being ripped out and going straight into a dark, wet cave to never come out again. Our fate is a dead end. A no-win.

The best moments of my life, I think, are where I am now. Still hanging on. But don't be fooled; there's nothing relaxing about my right now. Hanging on up here is like standing in the middle of the storm before a hurricane. I mean to say, I'm having a hard time now, but I know it's going to get way worse. No matter how I consider this, I'm doomed, and there's no way to come out on top of it. I remember growing into this spot on the eyelid with so much enthusiasm. Now I look back and see that I was only so keen because I was *so* naïve. Of course I was enthusiastic—I had no reason and no knowledge not to be.

Sometimes she treats us right, like we should be treated, but those moments are rare and far between. Those are the moments I'd heard about that made me enthusiastic about being here. Especially when there were more of us hanging. She'll sometimes paint us with a tiny, spiky brush that dries hard and makes us stand up straight and strong. It makes me proud of the work I'm doing. This is what I meant when I say I get hard. Her painting used to be a rare treat, but it has happened a little more recently. I don't know why, but I'm not complaining. That black paint makes me feel pretty, and she doesn't pull on us so much when it dries. The paint is our armor, at least for a little bit.

I used to think I'd be hanging here for a long time. I thought the spot I'm rooted in would be my forever. I was eager to protect her eye from all the things, and I thought having other eyelashes around me would mean being surrounded by friends. Only now, too late, I see I was wrong about everything. My reality couldn't be more contrary.

She has a plan for when we've all been ripped or fall out. I've seen it myself: black, plastic lashes that adhere to her eyelid with some kind of sticky goop. They're fake, of course, and I expect they'll feel awkward. I've read the package, and I know that she's supposed to glue those excuses over the exact place I'm rooted. What she doesn't know is that the new lashes will hurt—I know they will—and she'll look like a clown. They'll be heavy, so she'll probably flap her lids around the same way she does when water gets in her eye. She *will* be a clown. The lashes are also made of flimsy, tiny plastic, so they're gonna be awkward, and there's no way they'll look as good as we do.

Did. Before we became so scarce.

I'm not just saying all this because I'm bitter about being replaced, but that might also be true. Mostly, I still care about her. Even if she doesn't treat us with tons of respect, I still have a soft spot for her and for what we could be. If we could only work together.

I still hope we can get back to normal again. We can be full and grow thick if we're only given a chance. That's what I mean when I say *work together*: give us a chance. Eyelashes are some of the things you don't miss until they're gone—like a computer charger or toilet paper. Unlike a charger or paper, though, you'll miss your eyelashes when you look in the mirror and realize how much better you'd look if we're all there. She's taking us for granted. At least that's how I feel. I've thought a lot about things she might have missed out on because she keeps us scattered and paltry. I think if there were more of us, maybe she could hold on to that boy she hangs around with. Maybe he would stop leaving her, making her cry, and giving us so much overtime. Maybe she'd look better when she looked in the mirror. And maybe she'd be happy.

She's gotta stop ripping us out.

Wednesday, November 27

"I haven't seen you before." It comes as an accusation, almost, from behind me. A voice I don't recognize. When I turn, a woman is walking slowly, casually, down the hallway outside my apartment door. She has a long, black ponytail and an outfit that says she could be coming from a workout. "Did you just move in?"

"About a month ago," I say. She seems confident, albeit investigative, in a way that makes me want her on my side. "I'm Madison."

"Rosemary," she says and nods once. "I live right there." She points to a door two down from mine. "By myself. My boyfriend sometimes comes around, but he doesn't live with me."

"I have a boyfriend too." I stop myself from saying, "*Mine also comes around sometimes, and we're happy together.*" I don't say that, though, because it's not true. Charlie and I didn't officially break up-I don't think-but the way he's acting hasn't given me a lot of confidence.

"That's great," I say instead. "I hope I'll run into him one day." That part is only kind of true, but it seems like the right thing to say. Being this version of sad means I can hardly stand being around other people-particularly the happy ones and especially the coupled ones.

"Yeah, you probably will." Rosemary smiles with big, white teeth. Her smile makes me feel a little less foolish. Two beats of hesitation, then, "Hey, do you want to hang out sometime?" She glances down the hallway of doors behind me. "I guess you live on this floor too. I'll be around this weekend."

"I'd like that," I say, so quickly I almost cut her off with my response. I'm still perfecting my *play-it-cool* operation. "I'll look at my calendar when I get in and let you know what works." False. I don't have plans-of course I don't. "Put your number in here," I say, handing her my phone with an open contact entry. "I'll text you when I get in."

"Cool." She enters her number and hands my phone back to me with that same smile. "Talk to you soon."

I give her my best smile, nod my head once, then turn around-just barely fast enough to hide my eyes filling with tears. I'm either jealous of her boyfriend or sad that I don't have anyone to tell about my new friend. And I'm annoyed that I have to deal with either.

Friday, November 29

Charlie canceled our meeting. He said something about needing to "help out a friend," but he could have just as easily made that up. This is familiar. I let myself get excited about something, then he crushes it down and makes me second-guess myself.

Manipulation, I think it's called. Something like that.

This time, though, I bought a wand of mascara before I was supposed to see him, and I had been practicing. I wanted to have it mastered so I'd look good when he saw me. But now, all I've done is open the packaging and render it non-returnable. I'm frustrated.

I don't even like coffee. He should have remembered that.

Jenna

My name is Jenna, but only because that's what I call myself. I don't think it matters very much. Last week I called myself Hillary, and I was Tammy when I was made. Tammy was the name of the woman who made me in the factory, Hillary was someone shopping in my aisle, and same with Jenna. I change my name about once a week, but I like Jenna. It might stick.

I used to live in a dark Box surrounded by friends. In most ways, it was perfect. I learned a lot about myself and my situation in there: I'm one of the bigger ones, size Super, and I shared the Box with Mediums and Smalls. Even though we were different sizes and personalities, we got along fine—how I imagine a sorority house would. We were pretty much positioned in the Box next to our same size, so finding a mate wasn't that hard. We were all crammed in together, though, so we all had to get along. It was fine. At one point, I tried to figure out the sizes of the ones leaving the Box so I could get a better idea of who would be chosen next, but that got way too complicated. I gave it up. My success in predicting the next to be taken wouldn't have made much difference, anyway; no matter what size we were, we were all stuck in that Box with no say in when we'd get out.

I had a lot of time to think in there but not much to think about. The others didn't talk or, surprisingly, care much about what was happening to them. It amazes me how they could just sit in that Box, waiting, with no interest in what they were waiting for. They either had a peace that I can be jealous of, or an ignorance that I've obviated. Whether higher or lower, I was on an entirely different level than the other tampons in that Box. I'm not mad about that.

There was an exception, though, and she was using the name Tina when I left. I don't know how Tina knew so much about the Outside, but she told us stories, mostly about what was going to happen once we were chosen. Tina was only a size Medium, but everyone listened to her because she had what we all wanted: answers. And she was the loudest.

She said we were in a Box "for the Cycle," and that's why we were different sizes. I'm still not completely sure what that means, but I do understand that the Cycle runs the show. Everything that happened to us was based on what the Cycle was doing and what the Cycle needed. During the Cycle, which happened about once a month, the ceiling of our Box opened several times a day, and one of us was taken Outside for work. Even without my research, I could kind of guess who was going to be chosen. There was a mere predictability to it: first the Supers, then the Mediums, then the

Smalls. That rhythm helped us anticipate our going which, again, took a lot of effort and didn't make much difference. In this business, once you're chosen, you're chosen. Like it or not, there you go.

Tina was the first Medium chosen after a wave of Supers that I wasn't picked for—for some reason. So I was around to see her go. It was nice to hang around a bit before my turn, but it did get lonely when most other Supers and my friend was gone. One thing I'll never forget is how excited Tina looked when she was being pulled through the ceiling and into the blinding light of the Outside. She had no idea what was actually ahead of her—none of us did. Looking back, we shouldn't have been so happy.

Long before Tina left, she told us what she knew about our work Outside: we were made for a job, and the job starts the same second we leave the Box. We were made to fight something called "the Red" and to protect our girl from it. She said the Red will be warm and comfy when we first encounter it, so I won't know it's bad at first. But the Red can be tricky.

I'm glad she told me that so I could be prepared. I would have fallen for it, no question. Back then, I would have fallen for anything.

"The Red will trick you with its warmth," she said. "Then it'll get cold, absorb into your body, and never come out." She said it smells really bad once it soaks in. The Red can't be trusted, Tina insisted, but I didn't think it was that serious. She used the word "molest" to describe its soaking in, but I thought she was being dramatic. Tina could be a bit of a drama queen. Looking back, I should have taken her more seriously.

Whether Tina was being a drama queen or not, she made me understand why everyone hates the Red so much and why our girl needs protection. I understood what I was getting into with my work, at least partly. She told me that I had a responsibility: hold back the Red for as long as I could. I knew it'd come at me from my all sides, it would be very comfortable, and it was going to hang around. But I also knew that I had to fight back.

When I was in the Box, I couldn't imagine life Outside. The other sizes felt that way too—we talked about it sometimes. Most of our days were spent in silence, but someone would speak up every once in a while. It was usually a Small, saying something naïve or something about being scared. That helped my anxiety a bit; at least I wasn't afraid. I knew it was only a matter of time until I was chosen and, truly, I was mostly excited about it. It did get lonely in the Box, but I was thankful for my extended time in there—I didn't feel ready when the other Supers were taken. I knew I was made for the work Outside, but I wasn't in any rush to start.

On the day I was finally chosen, the Box was nearly empty; all my peers—the Supers—were lifted through the ceiling during the previous Cycle, so I was the biggest tampon left in the Box. For some reason, that made me feel like I had to be a leader for the smaller tampons. The Box had been dark for a while, so I expected I wouldn't have to be for long. Another Cycle was about to begin. I liked being the biggest, so I even kinda hoped I had more time in there.

It happened in a blink:

The ceiling opened up, the light flooded in and, like I saw with my peers, I was grabbed by my top and lifted through the ceiling. Into the light. I had no chance to even salute my sisters on my way up and out. Tina was excited when she was lifted from the Box, but I wasn't nearly as confident. Actually, I was terrified. I think extra time in there made me too comfortable, and I lost sight of my purpose: to stop the Red. I was made to protect the girl, and I was finally getting to it.

Before Tina left, she told us that our bodies would expand to ten times the size they were in the Box to help us in the fight. For a long time, I was more excited about the expansion than anything else. Tammy from the warehouse had me twirled into a tight, thick pole and stuffed into a narrow, plastic applicator for my sale. The tight pole and plastic applicator were the only things I'd known at that point, so I didn't realize how uncomfortable they were until I was free from them. Now, after I've left the Box and been free for so long, I can't imagine being happy wound up tight like that.

Tina was right about a lot, but not all of it. I had to fight the Red, sure, but there was much more to it.

When I was lifted from the Box, I was launched—quite literally—through a tight gap and into a dark room for the fight. She was right that the Red would come from all sides and it would trick me by being comfy, but I had a minute to myself before that began. When I shot from that applicator, taut for a fight, I landed in a dark room and had a chance to get myself together before my body grew and before the Red came. Tina had told me about getting bigger, sure, but how much bigger I would get was her exaggeration; I only got twice my size, if even. That's not my complaint—any kind of expansion is an improvement from the tight twirl, and it did help with fighting the Red. I was a little bit let down at the same time, though.

As soon as my body swelled to double size, I was surrounded. My battle began. The Red was warm like I expected, and it was very comfortable for a few seconds—maybe ten. The warmth became part of me, soaking into my body like bathwater into a sponge. I loved every second of it. If that's what it's like to protect my girl, sign me up for a lifetime of service.

I knew those feelings wouldn't last forever, though, so I enjoyed the warmth until it turned cold. In this business, good and comfortable never last.

The Red was comfortable for a short time. Then it was gone, replaced by cold and hollow. That discomfort was joined by an almost rusty smell, getting stronger every second. The commotion of my discomfort snapped my attention back to the fight before me: soaking up every drop of the Red I could and guarding my girl against the upset that had become my essence. My only hope against the smell, the cold, and the Red was to remember what Tina told me back in the Box: "You won't have to fight alone for long, Hill, so hold out until one of us comes to help you."

My name was Hillary back then, for a couple of hours. She and some others nicknamed me "Hill," so it didn't last long.

Tina was wrong about that part, too. No one ever came.

I laid still in that room while my body soaked up the Red and I grew heavier. It became near impossible for me to move around. Not that I needed to move around much—just a wiggle every now and then—but it's a good option when my only job is to lie there and absorb. I was alone in that room, and time slowed down. Like when I was in the Box, I had a lot of time to think. And to overthink.

I'm thankful this next part is not my own account, but a Small named Karen told me about one of us, Rachel, who was left in her fight for too long. She was in it for a couple of days—so long that her room got infected and started switching from hot to cold, hot to cold. She said the rust smell turned to a throw-up smell, and it hurt to move around. Again, there's no need to move around too much, but that wiggle is a nice option. Karen said that if Rachel had been in for much longer, the infection would have killed our girl, and all of us would have been thrown away. Stuck in our plastic cases and tight twirls forever. I can't even imagine.

I'm not sure how Karen knew Rachel's story, but I don't have much choice but to believe it. Some others—mostly Smalls—got very nervous after hearing it, but I felt okay. All I could really do was hope that Rachel taught our girl a lesson.

She did, I guess, because my fight ended too early. There's just no doubt: I was lying in the room, absorbing, when she pulled me long before I was full of Red. I still had some fight in me. As uneasy as I felt when I first left the Box and started my fight, I made a complete turnaround by the time I was in it: I was actually bummed when I had to leave. There's nothing I could have done to stick around longer. Literally nothing. Once my string is pulled, I'm out of there. Rachel showed me how it could have been much worse, though, so I guess I should be thankful I was pulled too early instead of too late.

On my way out, my body squeezed back through the tight gap, into one second of blinding light, and slammed into another dark box. That's where I am now.

My body is bigger and heavier with Red this time, so it's a little different from being in the first Box with friends. Actually, it's a lot different from that Box; it's still dark and crowded here, but this one is much more spacious and suitable for my bigger body. I'm surrounded by all kinds of things I don't recognize, but no one seems up for conversation. The mood is much different in here. It's sleepier, more resigned.

I think I see another tampon I recognize—the Super chosen before me—but it's hard to be sure. When we're big and more filled with Red, everyone sort of looks the same. I called to her when I first arrived, but she didn't respond. That could also be because she changed her name to something else. She was sprawled out on a piece of napkin, and it looked like she was resting. I noticed white spots on her body, which means she was pulled out too early like I was. But that's just my guess.

I'm sharing personal space with all kinds of things in this box, and I'm still not entirely sure where I am. It smells really bad in here—worse than the rust and worse than I've ever smelled. This might be the throw-up Rachel talked about. The ceiling opens sometimes like the first Box I was in, so I get to see my surroundings in spurts: a glass, oval-type object lying under my string; bits of paper and tissues scattered randomly; and a squishy, brown ball lying diagonally behind me. I don't know what any of it is, and that makes me miss Tina even more. She would know. I miss having her to listen to, even if I did find out some of the things she said weren't true. I'm surrounded by a lot, but I feel very alone.

Tina didn't tell me about this part, but she did say we would get a second chance at fighting back the Red. I really hope she was right about that. I still have some fight left in me and I'm not full yet, so I think I'll get to go back in. If this box is some sort of a waiting room before round two, I'm A-okay with being in here. It's a throw-up-scented sacrifice, but I'm okay. This could always be worse.

Tina also said we'd get to help each other in the fight, but I guess she was talking about when we go back in. Or she was just wrong. If I do get to see the others in round two, I expect I'll see some old friends from the Box. Honestly, that's why I'm okay with waiting: I miss them, and I'm surprised by how much I do. We'll be able to swap stories about our fight, and I'll tell the others what *really* happens when they're chosen. I'm ready to go. I've been in here long enough, so my turn must be coming soon.

Just in case it is, I'm changing my name to Erin.

Wednesday, December 4

Hygiene is a hot topic for me, and it has been for as long as I can remember. I don't care as much about the cleanliness of the world around me-I know there's little hope in that-but more about my own cleanliness. I don't think that's anything extraordinary, either. A lot of people care a lot about their hygiene. Or if they don't, they should. Those people in the latter, the uncaring ones, are just gross. Unattractive.

The best part about my hygiene is how I can control it.

I control how many times I shower: at least once a day or at the end of my time outside.

I decide how long I brush my teeth: for at least three minutes, and as the very first and last steps of my routine.

I choose which pieces of clothing I wear in what situation: my "inside clothes" don't go outside, and nothing is worn without a wash.

And I manage how much time I preoccupy myself with it all: maybe more than others.

I sit in my hygiene's driver seat, except once a month when a metaphorical wrench is thrown my way. You can guess it: the wrench is my period. I have a strict routine for managing my menstrual cycle to make sure I get as much control as I can. On the front end, I keep a calendar to chart every symptom and every indication that my period is about to start. No surprises. That part is pretty typical for women, I think.

I limit my social activity during Period Week. I might be overdoing it with this one, but I'd rather not risk something embarrassing happening. It's not like I have loads of social plans to cancel, though, so this one is easy. Charlie is only *just* coming back around, and I don't have many friends yet. That part I'm still working on.

I don't let tampons stay up there for more than two hours before I change them out, and I know *that* part is unusual. Excessive. No one has told me as much because I don't talk about this with anyone else, but the box says they can stay in there for four to eight hours. I realize this is one of my *too much* things; but, in the name of hygiene, is there even such a thing?

The risk of my accidentally leaving it up there too long and my parts getting infected is too much to risk. It's just too much. What if I get distracted and forget to change it? If I fall asleep and completely forget it's in me when I wake up? I can't access a bathroom for the entire afternoon? There are hundreds more scenarios that all end in my consequence. The stakes are too high, and I don't mind giving this some extra attention. If changing a tampon a lot is the biggest inconvenience of being a grown woman living on my own, so be it. That's a small price to pay.

To add flame to the metaphorical fire of my period every month, there's also such a thing as changing my tampon *too often*, when it's not *full enough*. That also leads to infection. See the dilemma here? Wearing a tampon too long grows infection, and not leaving it in for long enough grows infection. If not for its obvious benefits of discretion and hygiene, I wouldn't waste one more unit of stress on them.

I'm trying to win my boyfriend back, though, and having a lump in my pants from a menstrual pad doesn't feel like the right move.

Wide Awake

When I was a young teenager and still learning about my menstrual cycle and my changing body, I came close to paying a consequence. *Close.* I forgot about a tampon I put in, and I forgot about it for a full day. I didn't get any kind of sickness or side effect from my mistake, but I promised myself I'd never make that mistake again. I researched a bit afterward-maybe to scare myself straight-and read about a girl who left her tampon in for four days. *Four days.* I'm not sure how anyone in their right mind could forget about their tampon so completely, but I guess she was just very distracted? That distraction made her sick, sent her to the hospital, and just about killed her.

That stupid girl's mistake taught me a lesson about tampons: change them and change them often. But not *too* often. Thank goodness I didn't learn all this the hard way. When my flow is heavy, I go as far as setting an alarm during the night to wake me up and change it out in the right increments. Call me radical, but you can't call me irresponsible. I don't want to go to the hospital and almost die like that other girl. Obviously, I don't.

I know my "time of the month" is normal and healthy, but I can hardly stand the thought of a bloody mess. Maybe that's understandable; maybe it's not just me. I've never asked. I'd rather change my tampons *too many* times a day instead of *not enough* times, so the mess won't have a chance to set in. My schedule has to revolve around my stream for a few days a month because of how often I change, but that's the sacrifice. I also just don't like the idea of my body hanging on to its old and cold blood. A little *obsession* is an okay tradeoff. I'm not hurting anyone.

Every little girl, I think, makes a list of what they want in their future boyfriend, spouse, whatever. Maybe boys do that, too, but I somehow doubt it. All the same, "good hygiene" has always been near the top of my list in some capacity. I can get over someone who hangs his towel on the rack crooked or doesn't take his shoes off at the front door, but not brushing his teeth twice a day and not soaping up in the shower are deal-breakers. I can and I have looked past those things in a boyfriend, but I'm not as willing when I'm with someone whose husband-material. You get it: I don't want to live the rest of my life overlooking the disgusting habits-or non-habits-of "my person."

If you squint your eyes and see it my way, my *caring too much* and being a *helicopter*, like Charlie charges, only means I see potential in him. I don't know how he doesn't see that.

None of that matters now, though, because Charlie and I are Off, and again I'm alone. I live by myself, I'm taking care of myself, and I'm alone. When I'm feeling particularly strong, that's good enough. I'm not going to be alone forever, God willing, so I'm using this time to become the best version of me-for myself and for Charlie. The other times, when I'm feeling particularly weak and wrapped in my aloneness, I can't walk across the living room without crying.

That back-and-forth is exhausting: "I'm a *good person,* and anyone who can't see that is missing out." In the same breath: "But if I'm so *good*, why am I alone so much?" Stronger Madison is fed up with Weaker Madison. That's not a surprise.

Everyone has *things,* but at least mine are simple. They're demanding of me and enormously time-consuming, but they're harmless. I try to frame some of my *things*-my tampon compulsion, for example-as a habit of taking care of myself so I won't get so irritated with myself. I expect other people won't see them that way, so it's better that I keep mostly to myself. Heaven help me if Charlie ever found out about all my *extra*.

You know what, though? Why would he find out? Boys don't like to talk about that kind of stuff, anyway. I don't have to talk about my period or my tampons with anyone. That's what this journal is for. I understand now.

Friday, December 13

"I've been thinking about what you told me at lunch," Mom says as soon as I answer the phone. "Why don't we go shopping next week? We can get some stuff for your apartment, then maybe look at some clothes after."

We met for lunch on Tuesday and I tried to keep up my *life-is-great-and-I'm-so-happy* act for as long as I could, but she saw through it. Hiding something from her is an almost-lost cause. I dropped it before we even got our drinks and I told her I'm miserable.

I didn't tell her the truthful *why* I'm out of sorts, though. I said I didn't know many people in my building yet and that I'm still getting used to living by myself, but I didn't admit that Charlie and I are nearly shipwrecked. That would only make her worry and come to my emotional rescue. And that's just too much right now. I'm not strong enough to talk about him yet, especially to my mom in public. So I played my other cards: I miss my college friends, and I don't feel *home* yet. It was believable, and not entirely untrue.

"How does that brown table look in your bedroom?"

"Bad," I say. "But I put it on the other side of my kitchen counter. I keep my avocados in that green bowl you gave me. It works."

"Good," she says. "Good idea." I can hear her doing something, some moving around, in the background of our conversation. "Okay, just calling to check-in. Give me a call later."

"I will," I say with the enthusiasm back in my voice. It was genuine now, though, because talking to her made me feel better. Even if I still feel stuck in my low-lit apartment surrounded by things that remind me of him, pretending like nothing is wrong helps. A combination of both makes me feel like I'll make it to the other side of this. "I love you, Mom."

"I love you too, sweetie," she replies. "Talk to you soon."

Monday, December 16

I've always been different, ever since I can remember. I wasn't different like the kid who sat next to me in science that read Japanese comics and smelled like Styrofoam; I was different because I didn't pay attention in class, I never finished my schoolwork, and my grades were always my greatest struggle. I adopted a slew of behaviors and habits to accommodate my difference that no one could make sense of, not even me. Thankfully, though, according to my classmates, I was different in a *cool* way.

My miseries showed up to my peers as my rebellion, and they joined me. They named me their ringleader, but I didn't ask for that. My parents didn't share their enthusiasm around my defiance, so I spent a chunk of my childhood in Time Out, or banished to my room without TV privileges on weekend afternoons. Thankfully, at least with my classmates, my deviations only made me *cooler*. More rebellious. Back then, anyway, my *disinterest* was serviceable to my social status. So I had a lot of friends to cushion my difference.

I got away with all that when I was a kid, but now I'm grown. Growing up hasn't changed much about my mental state, but now there's no one around to put an attractive label on it. I've just had to learn how to accommodate my differences and blend in a little better. But certain things still hold me back.

I made an appointment with my doctor last week because I have a hard time focusing on my work. When I started my job from home, it became apparent how constantly, *constantly* distracted I'll get when I'm trying to get something done. Even simple stuff. I'm not particularly interested in the work I do, so I used that as my excuse for a long time. But my wandering and sometimes an absence of mind happen too often to justify. It's irritating, even to me. No sooner do I read an email and hit Reply, my mind will switch to what I have to do after I hit Send, what I'll eat for dinner, then my weekend plans. It has become near impossible to get anything done because my mind keeps losing its train. It's like I'll start doing something with the best of intentions, then have no flippin' idea what I was doing a moment later. For the most part, I've been able to work around my deviations because, well, I'm used to them. But my lack of focus is getting in the way of my job, so I had to do something.

My boss even told me to "go see a doctor, Madison." Okay, insulting? But I am. I'm doin' it.

I've done a lot of research on myself and my habits, and I've landed on a diagnosis. I found a disorder that fits my description, and it even has a solution: take a pill and be done with it. I know what's wrong with me, so now I just need to convince a doctor so I can get a prescription.

Enter Dr. Glen Miller, my general practitioner. Doctors' first names have always felt like a well-kept secret, so I've always made a point to learn them, then throw them out every once in a while. Just for spice.

Glen.

I did my due diligence before meeting with Dr. Miller-of course I did-and I was armed with what I thought was the answer to who and how I am: attention deficit hyperactivity disorder, or ADHD. I told him about my *things* and why I thought ADHD was a good fit. He listened to what I had to say through squinted eyes and a few rare nods of his head.

"On a scale of one to five, how often do you have trouble finishing a project once the challenging parts have been done?" *Five.*

"When you have a task that requires a lot of thought, how often do you avoid or delay getting started?" *Five.*

"When something unexpected happens, what is your stress level around that event?" *Five.*

"How often do you feel overly active or compelled to do things, like you're driven by a motor?" *Five.*

There were a few more questions, but the mood of my answers was the same: affirmative. Every answer I gave sent him in a flurry of scribbles on his clipboard, but the flurries didn't make me too nervous. They probably said something in the order of: "Bingo-ADHD."

Dr. Miller asked more questions about my behavior in certain situations, other people's experience with me, my symptoms, and about my performance in school. Most of his questions seemed irrelevant-I didn't understand how a lot of them were related to my diagnosis-and it took a long time to answer them all. The whole time I talked, though, he kept scribbling notes, then drawing circles around his scribbles. When his pen stopped moving, he looked up with a solemn face.

"This sounds a lot like ADHD." He looked down at the paper with the circles on it. "But I'll run more tests before I can be sure." He looked up from his paper and locked onto my eyes. He was keeping up the solemn charade, which I appreciated. "I'm going to step out for a minute, then someone will come in and take you to our testing room."

I nodded my head, and he stood up to leave. I'm not sure what deemed the room we were in a "regular room" and the other a "testing room," but I didn't care enough to ask. Instead, I sat and waited. Less than one minute later, as if she was waiting outside the door, a little head peeked in.

"Follow me, sweetie," a tall woman with a Southern accent announced. She led me down a hallway and to another room. This one *was* different. I could see that. It was empty except for a small table, two metal chairs, buzzing fluorescent lights, and what felt like an air conditioner blowing directly on us.

The word *uncomfortable* comes to mind. It was very uncomfortable. The "testing room."

Dr. Miller reappeared through the door, just as the Southern woman had. "Thank you, Betty," he said, and the woman nodded away. He took a seat across from me and laid down a stack of folders. "Each of these activities will test a different area of your cognition. This is the last step before I can give you a diagnosis. Ready to get started?"

Dr. Miller and I sat in that cold and uncomfortable room for another hour. Each of his activities measured my ability to focus on tasks, to remember details over a period of time, my tendency to forget objects when they're not present in front of me, and a few more that I didn't get a chance to understand. It was stressful, exhausting, and I didn't enjoy myself at all. But the reward of my *normalcy*, for Charlie's sake, makes it worth the trouble.

"That's all for today," Dr. Miller looked up at me and said after scribbling a few more things on his paper, drawing a few more circles. "I've treated a lot of people with ADHD, so there's nothing to be embarrassed about." His eyebrows relaxed, and his expression changed from sympathetic to suggestive. But I wasn't embarrassed. Why would I be embarrassed? I'm the one who gave him the ADHD idea in the first place. "I'll take a closer look, then someone from our office will be in touch."

That last part-his abrupt shutdown of my appointment without giving me a diagnosis-was maddening. Time is money I guess, though, and my summation hadn't been short.

"Thank you," I stood up and mumbled on the way through his office door.

Despite the ambiguity of my appointment with Dr. Miller, I spent the two days I waited for a callback to convince myself that I did, in fact, have ADHD. I'd like to think of myself as an *accomplished* late-night researcher and self-diagnoser, and I was sure about this one. So when someone called me about it two days later, I wasn't surprised.

"Hello, Ms. Madison," a sweet-sounding woman said on the other end of the phone. I figured I wouldn't get a call from Dr. Miller himself, but from one of his nurses. It's okay. "Dr. Miller reviewed your file, and he called in a prescription for Adderall. You have ADHD."

"Thank you," I said, trying to sound sweet in return. The diagnosis blew over me easily because I had already taken a few weeks to let it sink in. The extra layer of sweet was the satisfaction of my correct diagnosis. Call me Dr. Madison, without the paycheck.

I know some things I do are illogical-people have used that against me my whole life. Acquiring this diagnosis was only to give me a defense for it. In more than one of our arguments, Charlie reminded me that I'm *too much*. But I don't know what to be sorry for-I just like things a certain way, done in a certain order, and in a certain place. Doesn't everyone? I think my *things* are normal, but Dr. Miller's diagnosis confirms otherwise. I think the reasoning behind all of them is just common sense; I can, and I did, explain them away for as long as I've been aware. I think my *things* are just like everyone else's *things*. I guess I'm wrong, though. Apparently, doctor diagnosed, Charlie was right: I am, can be, *too much*.

But too much for whom? I use my habits and tendencies to get through my life on my terms. As long as my rituals help me adapt and function in the world, what's the harm? I like pictures on the wall to be straight, and I take pride in being a precisian. So what if I'm a little persnickety along the way?

My new diagnosis forces me to reflect on myself a lot. Particularly about the time I was in elementary school and how much I hated reading aloud. I remember knowing that something wacky happened with my comprehension when the teacher called on me to read, and I remember the spasm of anxiety it sent me into, but I never knew the reason behind it. I was so young. Now, in light of my diagnosis, it makes so much sense. Research says it's common for kids with ADHD to struggle with focus, processing, and management when they (we) read aloud.

None of us knew about my "sickness" at the time, so, again, my refusal was labeled as my rebellion.

I annoyed over that particular activity enough to earn me a pass when my teacher chose narration for text. My friends saw my wavering as *cool* defiance, and they followed suit. With most of the class behind me, our teacher had such a hard time finding someone to read that she gave up trying; she would either read aloud to us herself, or she told us to "read it in your head." Which, okay, but no one ever did. It's fine.

My teacher confirmed my ringleader status after that first incident, and it held up for most of my years in lower school. Where I was accommodating my needs and what I now know as my disability, my peers saw me as their champion. I don't know if I'm proud or ashamed of that fact, but I think I can be proud. I know it now and I had a hunch then: if I ever hope to work around them, I have to prioritize my differences to the spotlight. When I was young and still figuring myself out, I didn't get the choice to blend in like the other kids did. Thank goodness I was *cool*.

My variations at that age were justified with words like "unique" or "remarkable." They further validated me with words like "quirky" and "eccentric," so I had no reason to look into them any harder.

A better word to use: denial. And perhaps a little foreshadowing.

There is still a bit of denial in me, still a large piece that wants to believe that my mind is healthy. *Normal*. Even for a diagnosis as common and beyond my control as ADHD, I was in denial for a few weeks after receiving that call from Dr. Miller's office. I convinced myself that everyone has *things,* and there's nothing at all special about mine. Maybe mine are more outwardly and they get more in the way sometimes, but all my *things* are harmless. The only things I'm hurting, if we're going to call it that, are myself and my time.

I have a hard time dealing with stress, but who doesn't?

Who cares if I can't multitask?

I can't focus sometimes, but how about you be more interesting?

I'm coming around to it slowly, but also with all the time in the world. Heck, I would be okay to never accept my diagnosis and keep living in the bubble of my disability for the rest of my life. That last one is tempting; you know it is. But I did come around, and I did what I was told: I filled the Adderall, and I started taking the pills as prescribed. Two to three every day, with food. I was good about taking them because I wanted to get better-for myself and for Charlie. I'll never admit it to him, but he was right when he told me, "There's something *wrong* with you, Madison."

Oh man, that made me angry. He said those words with such hate in his voice, and I received them that way. Like a knife in my gut. A part of me was also embarrassed. His words dug that knife deeper into my side, then twisted it counterclockwise, leaving me to hide the blood. He can be so nasty to me, then at the same time claim to care. I grew angry. Resentful.

But now I see he was right. *Lesson learned.*

An ADHD diagnosis explains a few things, and it gives justification for some things that drive Charlie crazy. A part of me wants to call him up and either say, "See? It's not my fault," or "I'm getting better. Give me another chance." I can't do that, though, because Charlie and I still aren't talking. I'm figuring all this out too late.

Charlie or not, ADHD answers some big ones for me: why I was so behind in school, why I had so much trouble concentrating, and why I never could finish my classwork. There were a lot of "AHAs," but there was still a dump of unanswered questions following behind me: ADHD doesn't explain the constant commotion in my head. It doesn't explain why I brush every tooth with a fetish before bed every night or my over-occupation with controlling everything and every person in my life. It doesn't explain why I can't move forward in my thoughts until I yank at and remove almost every follicle on my eyelid. Other people see me as hyperactive and distractible, but I see a hurricane perpetually touching down.

The symptoms of what I now know as ADHD started slowly, making them easier to substantiate and normalize into my routine. And easier to ignore. My first indication was my inability to read aloud in grade school, then it grew into my irritation with trivial things like what size pen I use and when. That one has stuck around. My list of habits and compulsions has gotten longer with every year that passes because, somehow, I've gotten worse over time. Sicker. Not one second goes by that my mind is not in absolute chaos.

My difference, now I know as my *disorder,* is every day pushed closer to the spotlight.

I think about my diagnosis as a way out. If my treatment is as simple as taking a pill a couple times a day to make me a peaceful, more relaxed-minded person, I can do that. Major bonus if it also makes me a better girlfriend to Charlie. He stood beside me the whole time I was *wrong* and untreated, so taking a pill is the least I can do. For him and for myself, this is my step one.

Tuesday, December 17

BLING . . . BRIIING . . .

BLING . . . BRIIING . . .

"Hello?" I run to my phone and answer it without looking at the name on my screen. It has been a slow morning at work, and the quiet of my apartment is particularly suffocating.

"Hey," someone, a vaguely familiar female voice, says. "It's Rosemary. Your neighbor." She doesn't know she's my only friend-if I can call her that-so there's no way I'd lose context.

I play it *cool*, though. Sometimes I can be.

"Oh," I say. "Hey. How's it going?"

"I'm good-just checking in." Her voice is casual, almost uncaring. I try to match it. "I haven't seen you around much, so I wanted to make sure you're still alive over there."

"I'm good," I say with a forced laugh. She hasn't seen me around because, these days, I don't leave my apartment except for the grocery store. But that's my secret. "I haven't been feeling great lately, so I was lying low."

Not a full lie; feeling *sad* isn't feeling *great*. There's technically some truth to it.

"Ah, boo," she says. She's genuine, which makes me feel good. "How are you now?"

"I'm better today," I say. Talking to her is making me feel better, so that also isn't a full lie. "Hey, do you want to hang out sometime? I'll be around this weekend."

"That's what I was calling about," she says. "I picked up a bottle of wine at the grocery store yesterday in case you're free. Come over Friday night?"

"That works," I say casually, not to give away my excitement. "How about five-thirty? I'll bring crackers or something."

"Perfect," she said. "Five-thirty works."

She hangs up without saying "bye," "looking forward to it," or "I'm excited about you." But it's okay. Those parts are implied.

For a few minutes after she's gone, I stand there, smiling. I pick up a pen, write "cracker, cheese" on a notepad hanging on my refrigerator door, and skip-walk back to my living room. Maybe a friend is what I need to get me out of the slump Charlie put me in. Rosemary might do the trick.

Prashant

I'm the biggest of all my friends; I know I am. We've sat next to each other to compare our sizes, and I always win. I'm proud of that. I like being the biggest because it means I get the most action. There's a girl who comes to see me two, three times a day, and that's waves more than the others can say. I'm proud, but I'm not conceited.

She puts a lot of different things inside me: sometimes cool and sometimes lukewarm, but mostly hot things. The hot can be intense and uncomfortable, but, for the most part, it's predictable. I might even say it's boring. It's boring in the same way that being burned alive regularly is boring. Now you see what I mean?

To be clear: I'm a cup, a drinking cup, and my name is Prashant. I can hold twenty-two ounces of liquid, so I'm pulled more often than the other sizes, but it doesn't get much more exciting than water, milk, sometimes soda, and tea. The cool and lukewarm can also be kinda boring because, again, they're predictable. The girl who uses me is on a routine: one fill of water in the morning, milk around lunchtime, hot tea in the late afternoon, water or soda in the evening, and another cup of tea, steaming hot and filled to my brim, before bed. Give or take another fill of tea on some days—her thirsty ones, I guess.

The hot tea fills are my least favorite of the day, no matter how many I live through. You'd think I'd be numb by now, but I'm not. The only thing I'm numb to is the repetition and the predictability of my existence. The discomfort or numbness of the burn, though? Certainly not. At least not yet. Part of me thinks I might never get used to that.

I spend all day, every day, dreading the hot part. But it always comes.

It's the afternoon right now as I'm telling this, and she has already filled me to my nearly top edge with cold water. The cold is step one of this routine that I go through several times every day but, still, it hits me like a jolt. It's an expected jolt so it's *fine,* but it's still a jolt. I used to get very anxious around this point because of what I know comes after the cold, but I'm more relaxed about it these days. That's the predictability I'm numb to. *Bored of.*

After she fills me with cold, she carries me to a Locker of some sort. And my disquiet begins. Inside the Locker, there's a podium she'll set me on, then she closes the door, and I'm in complete darkness. It's always pitch black for at least another second before a string of very loud beeps erupts in the air around me. The beeps are fast and they go away quickly enough that I barely register them, but they immobilize me just the same. It's not like I have much in the way of mobility anyway, but you know what I mean.

The beeps stop, always suddenly, then the lights come on like a Christmas show. The Locker comes alive.

DROMP.

A noise like a thunder crash—just one—echoes around me, followed by a *hmmm* so loud it rattles my water. One time, the *hmmm*s rattled me so much that the water spilled over my rim and onto the podium beneath me. I sat in a puddle of my own bowels for the rest of that Locker session, until she opened the door and cleaned them off my sides and the surface where I sat. That was humiliating and a little bizarre. I felt like I was soaking in a part of myself that I should have never even had to see.

I think she learned her lesson from the spill because she doesn't fill me up so much anymore. I don't get so full that I have reason to concern much over my overflow; the *dromp* and *hmmms* are my only upsets. Those noises I can handle, though, because they don't physically strike me. Or maybe I can handle them because I'm already struck.

The humming continues for two full minutes but, sitting in the bright Locker where my insides grow in pressure and blaze against me, two minutes feels like thirty.

A lot of things happen next, and I don't know what to tell you is the most offensive. I *can* say, though, that the temperature of my body is the worst of it. The process always starts with something innocent—the cold water. Then the Locker changes it to something evil; my ice-cold becomes searing hot and wicked by the time I come off that podium.

The *hmmms* make my water smell like plastic, but it somehow stays bland and flat. The taste of the water changes too. Like spit, but only sort of.

Telling my story like this puts it in a perspective I haven't had before. It all sounds like something I could rage over. The girl, whoever she is, swoops me up and violates me with a shock of cold. She sets me on a plastic podium in a stainless-steel prison, where she locks me inside and scalds the sense out of me. But maybe that's just it. I don't even have the sense to be mad about it. I'm so focused—I have to be—on preserving myself that I don't even have a sense of justice. I'm just trying to get through this.

The next thing I can count on (it happened this time too) is for her to reach into the Locker and drag me back to the cool of the outside. You might think the cool would be a liberation for my steaming body but, as I said, I don't comprehend much at this point. Maybe it is, or maybe it makes the pain worse. Really, I dunno.

Now as I'm saying this, I've just been dragged from the Locker. And I'm burnin'. The burn makes everything around me fall into the background because my pain demands all my comprehension. I'm trying to stay alert, though, so I can tell my story.

boomp.

A small metal ball drops into my water with a smaller splash. This part still surprises me, despite its happening every time she burns me hot. At least twice a day. The drop is so slight that it could probably go unnoticed but, again, I've been around this block before. That ball is the fulcrum of the tea-making process, so I'm better about expecting it now.

The ball has pieces of dirt in it that drop into my water, float around, and are very much trapped. The pieces smell like what they are—dirt—and they don't say anything. They never do. They just float in their ball and soak up my water until they swallow enough of it, I guess, to grow into small, blanket-like pieces. My water's blandness turns bitter and metallic, but it still smells like dirt. Those blankets must have some control over my water's shift, but that's just my guess. At the very least, the dirt pieces are a distraction from my burning agony, so I appreciate them. I don't necessarily understand the magic behind them, but I don't think she could make tea without them.

The only exciting part about this operation—if I can even call it "exciting"—is watching what color I'll turn after the dirt grows to blankets. My water is turning dark brown right now, for this round, but before I've become a foggy shade of clear, a very light brown, and once a tiresome shade of pink. Most often, though, I turn some shadow of brown. My color has something to do with the dirt she puts in me, but I haven't figured out the specifics.

Calling any part of my scorching burn "exciting" is like calling a contraction "the peaceful part" of childbirth. That is, my color change is the best part of an overall agonizing situation—necessary, but still agonizing.

The process is the same in the afternoons as at bedtime, but the afternoons hit me harder for some reason. Even when the worst part is over and the blankets are bouncing around, I can't help but fixate on my next fill. I'm way too hot, and the only way to pass the time in my purgatory is to hope for the water to spill from my sides or for my body to split open. At least then I would get some relief from the heat. I'm wishing for my own ruination, I realize that, but those consequences don't really register while I'm boiling like this. All I can do is think about my immediate relief.

I don't know how else to tell you how uncomfortable this is, except to describe the steam that rolls from my rim. It's like blood gushing from a wound. I think that's good enough imagery. My base is blistering from the temperature of my body at this point, and I'm helpless in my own mitigation. All I can do is sit here on the countertop, screaming. No one can hear my screams, but they make me feel better.

Hardly. Please believe that when I hold boiling water or hot tea, my screams don't stop.

What goes up must come back down. In the same way, what's boiling hot has to cool back down. That's also what happens to me; I start to cool. Eventually, the water that fills me will return to its cooler temperature, but it's never soon enough. My cooling is slow and tingly, and it feels like a slow-burning victory. Like coasting down a steep hill that I've just bicycled up. Mine is a slow coasting that never gathers any speed, though, like my bike can't disengage its brakes.

When I cool down, the light at the tunnel's end turns back on, and I see my hope.

When I reach a temperature that's not scalding but still steaming, she usually picks me up and blows her warm breath on me. For some reason. The warmth of her mouth's air doesn't have much use except maybe to make her feel good, but it doesn't do any harm, either. She'll take a few slurps off my top, then sometimes drop a cold cube in me—much like the metal dirt ball, but I like this drop better. The cube melts within seconds of coming in and helps my cooling a little bit. A tiny, tiny bit.

First, she slurps, then she takes me places. I've only ever traveled to rooms in her house, but I get to see the big, big world inside these walls. When she fills me in the morning, I sit alongside a sink in her bathroom while she gets ready. I go to her desk in the afternoon, where she'll light a candle and hang out for a while. Then she takes me to the sofa in the evenings while she watches TV or reads a book. That last part is usually just the two of us, but sometimes she eats with a friend. A boy. I don't know what's going on with that.

And that's the normal routine. Right now, though, I'm still sitting next to the Locker, smelling like plastic and with steam still rolling from my top. The steam is wearing down because I'm losing heat with every passing second, and I'm getting more anxious with every wasted degree. I'm helpless on this table, which puts me very much on edge. Where is she, but also . . . why did I just live that agony for no purpose?

And worst of all, I'm helpless.

I wait and I wait for her to come back for me. I don't know how long I've been sitting on this counter waiting, but it feels like a lifetime. In a few ways, it *is* a lifetime, because I don't think those blankets are reusable—my boiling water is all they have. I don't mind the part where I'm getting cooler so much because it means there's some relief coming at me. My cooled water is comfortable in the same way that milk, soda, or water is comfortable. Like when a sunburn heals or a bad haircut grows back.

I'm becoming more comfortable now that I've been sitting here a while, but I'm still not sure what I'm waiting for. That's the most aggravating part of all this. I'm starting to think I've been made—brewed—and forgotten, but a small part of me still has hope this wasn't a mistake. She might be trying to drink cold tea for some reason, and my chill is intentional. My hope, really, is all I have. All I can do right now is sit on the counter, cool off, and wait for my next move. At least I'm not burning anymore.

"*Oh*!" I hear her voice after an hour, it seems, of losing heat. My water is closer to room temperature, which I like, but it isn't quite to *comfortable* yet. Her voice sounds more relaxed than I would have hoped after one hour of my whole neglect. But I hear some relief. "Oh, my gosh."

In one forgotten second, she picks me up by the handle on my backside and lifts me to her mouth. Twenty seconds pass and with one continued gulp, she drains all twenty-two ounces of me. Like an animal. It's gross, but I'm frustrated, so everything is painted a shade darker. She emptied me of that awful liquid, at least until next time. The only good thing about her leaving me to cool almost *all the flip down* is, undeniably, that she can drain me straight away.

I'm one of the biggest cups, but that comes with responsibility: I'm constantly on the job, and I don't get much downtime. Almost none. In the same minute, I'm voided, she walks me straight over to the sink, fills me with soap, then leaves me to soak until my next fill—in a few hours, probably. I know the hot stuff is coming again soon, but she usually gives me a reprieve of water (or soda) before another hot. There are a few things I don't like about the soda—the bubbles, for one—but it pales in comparison to the burn. I've actually grown to appreciate any alternative. I'm taking the good with the bad, though, so I'm okay with it. Whatever she wants, it's fine.

I guess I don't care what she puts in me very much, but that's mostly because I don't have the *ability* to care. I'm her go-to for all the uncomfortable stuff, but I'm also her biggest and favorite. At the end of the day (or the beginning, or the middle), whatever she wants, I'm here to help her get it in. My name is Prashant, and I'm just a cup. Her favorite cup, no less. Sometimes, I need the reminder.

I'm exhausted, well-worn, and slightly brown-tinted, but I'm her favorite. And that's good enough for me. It has to be.

Friday, December 20

I've never been a fan of medicine, not really, and I'm not inclined to take any doctor's advice as an absolute the first time I hear it. The medical community is full of smart people, but even smart people make mistakes. I guess what I'm saying is I'm still in a bit of denial about my diagnosis.

I'm proud of the fact that I don't have a lineup of pills to take every morning because that makes me feel *normal*. My medicinal independence is my freedom, and I'm trying to hold on to it for as long as I can. Not taking a bunch of pills means I spend a lot of my time and effort on the extra work it takes to preserve my body and mind. Still, though, I'm hit with this attention-deficit crap.

I'm okay to take a pill for a little while, but ultimately, I want to fix myself on my own terms-not Dr. Miller's. But I just don't know how. So, I asked the internet. And I'm sure that's nothing remarkable.

I researched, checked sources, and read a novel-worth of articles on DIY cures to my mind's malfunction. I passed through my denial and my "I can fix myself" phase and I was looking for a non-prescription approach to managing my brain's shortcomings. My *things*. I was looking for a way to show up as *normal* to my peers, to blend in with them, and maybe even befriend a few. These years are supposed to be the "best of my life," so if that means I have to accommodate a couple new habits to keep my disorder under the blanket while I find my community, so be it. That's a sacrifice I can make.

Where Dr. Miller wants to fix me with an Adderall prescription and talk therapy, I decided to meet him halfway: I'll take the pills, but I'm not going to therapy to talk about my *things*. In place of therapy, I drink hot tea.

Hear me out: Research found that caffeine reduces the severity of attention deficit hyperactive symptoms. It's typically used as an *auxiliary* treatment for ADHD. So I'm using it as such; I'm drinking tea, *and* I'm taking my pills. I don't feel like I need a lot of extra help because it's not like I've been crippled in everyday tasks. Or like I was hurting anyone. But I'm open to the help.

I'm getting healthy for myself and for Charlie.

I have some pretty well-toned self-diagnosis and DIY-treatment muscles, and I just wanna see how far they'll take me. I'm taking the Adderall as Dr. Miller prescribed-mostly to my chagrin-and I'm using my muscles to find something that'll supplement it. Something to make the pills work faster and eventually replace them altogether. Hopefully not *too* eventually, though. One day, in my dreams, my treatment will look like my dropping the pills and just drinking a few cups of tea every day. My disorder gives me a chance at a real-life Pavlovian experiment-classical conditioning at its finest. Coming off the pills and only drinking tea to calm my disordered brain is my dream, and doesn't it sound nice? Simple, *normal*.

I don't have to do much in the way of accommodation to incorporate hot tea into my routine; I've drunk it for a while, and I like it okay. I've just had to fine-tune a couple of things: I bought the biggest mug I could find, a twenty-twoouncer; I set a schedule to keep my caffeine consumption at its height; and I steep loose leaf tea leaves in steaming water for a minimum of six minutes—all the things the internet said will give the highest caffeine output. This is my ADHD treatment on a *budget*, so I'm all about enhancing those affordable resources.

Mostly I drink tea, but an occasional soda isn't out of the question. Too much sugar gives me a headache, though, so I drink soda only as a treat. I tried coffee for about two weeks when I worked my first job out of college, but I stopped when I couldn't grow a taste for it. Back then, I got caught in the peer pressure of everyone around me claiming to "need coffee before I can function," from its delicious but sugar-heavy creamer that I doused my coffee in ("some coffee with your creamer, Madison?"), and from my company's giving it to employees for free. At the end of those two weeks, I recognized that the tiny bit I enjoyed the coffee was not even worth the extra trip to the bathroom. It was a good effort, if not a quick one.

So now, enter hot tea. Especially in light of my diagnosis, my research, and my self-imposed caffeine quota, I love it. As much as a person can love a drink, anyway. And I can throw it back too.

Writing it that way makes me sound much more exciting and dangerous than someone who just *loves drinking tea*, but that's what I'm going for: to make it seem better than it is. Because if I don't do that, I'd have to go to talk therapy.

I drink all kinds of teas (white, herbal, green, chai, oolong), but I mostly like it black. Black tea has the most caffeine, okay, but I also like its strong flavor. I drink at least two cups of the twenty-two-ounce mug per day, give or take one more when I'm bored at work. It's an easy habit to make-and to hold on to-and if it's also helping my disordered mind, to fill me up. I drink other things, of course I do, but outside of tea, there isn't much room in my body for more liquid. Water, milk, sometimes soda-all the *normal* stuff. Some parts of me still are.

There's no way to measure how much or how little my caffeine intake is helping my ADHD, but I'm optimistic. I can talk about the one time I was able to sit at my desk and focus on my writing for a few hours or the time I didn't beat myself up over leaving my bathroom light on, but that "progress" could also be my wishful thinking. My mind, I'm learning, is an exceedingly powerful weapon. I'm trying to outsmart it away from its disorder, and caffeine is just one attempt. It would be great if drinking an extra cup alongside one Adderall pill is enough to make the difference, but I'm still doing my research. Just upping my caffeine is a very charming treatment for a wearing condition that affects my every day, so it might be too easy and too good to be true. But I have to try. I'm doing everything I can to be good-for Charlie and for myself.

As for the talk therapy, I'm apprehensive, so I'm holding off. I don't have much faith in a therapist telling me something I haven't already read about and tried, so it'll be my last resort.

Can't this be that simple? Dr. Miller prescribed a pill and therapy for my diagnosis, and I'm meeting him halfway. Or

I'm only *going* halfway. I want to take my shot at my own natural approach to a cure before I give myself over to the medication + therapy cocktail. I'm stalling my slip underwater and into the mainstream.

It makes perfect sense to me. Caffeine just happens to be an easy place to start.

Sunday, December 22

"Madison." Rosemary says my name when she opens the door to her apartment-in lieu of "hello" or "nice to see you," I guess. Her unorthodox doesn't surprise me anymore. It's refreshing. She turns on her heel and leads me into her living room. "I think our apartment layout is the same, so welcome home, pretty much."

"Thank you," I say with a laugh-maybe harder than is justified. "I don't remember putting this here." I pick up a pillow on the couch and fake-examine it. Not my best humor, but she laughs anyway.

"My boyfriend just left so we can have 'Girl Time,'" she says with air quotes and a small eye roll. "He works the night shift, though, so he was just going to work."

I respond with a smaller, more appropriately sized laugh and a smile across my face. She told her boyfriend about me, enough for him to give us time to hang out. That simple act makes me feel wanted, recognized, and appreciated for the first time in a while.

"What does he do?"

"He's a night nurse," she says. "The schedule sucks, but he loves it. Sometimes he comes here to nap during the day, so that's usually when I see him."

I give her a look and nod that communicates something like, "That's a bummer." But I'm feeling the exact opposite: I want a boyfriend to come to my house-if only to nap-and I wish I had someone I could tell about *my* new friend. I don't say that, though, because it would blow my cover. Also, too much boyfriend talk might make her ask about Charlie again. I change the subject.

"I love how you've decorated the place," I say. Rosemary has a random, colorful style that translates to brightly colored blankets, pillows of abstract shapes, and vases of large, fake flowers.

"Thanks," she says. "All the flowers are fake because I can't ever remember to water them. I have a *brown* thumb."

"I'm the same way," I reply. "I thought about getting a cat when I moved in here, but I can't even keep a plant alive. I can't be trusted with another life."

"Your boyfriend comes around some, right?" she asks. *Shoot*. "I keep missing him, but I also don't hang out in the hallway. Maybe I should so I can meet this guy."

"He travels a lot for work," I say. Another lie. "He gets back in a couple weeks, though, so I'll introduce you." Charlie and I will be good again in a couple weeks, surely. I think. If not, I'll have to make up another lie. This could get messy, but I think a couple weeks is safe.

"That'd be fun," she says and brightens back up. "We can go on a double date."

"Cool," I say with fake resolve. "He would like that too." My smile is too big, maybe, but I like the possibility. I'm *beaming*.

"Do you want some wine? I'll get you a glass from my cabinet," I say, changing the subject and continuing with the bad-but-successful joke from before.

She laughs again, so I'll call that "playing to my audience."

I walk into her kitchen, spin around, and open a door above the sink: bingo. An apartment-sized kitchen means there are only a few options for storage, so my odds were pretty good. "What do you do for work?" I ask, filling the glasses halfway, then carrying them to where she stands. I hand her one, my confidence still sailing.

"Oh, it's nothing exciting," she says, "but it pays the bills. I work at the front desk at a chiropractor's office. I've always wanted to do something in healthcare, but I never wanted to go to school for it."

"Ah, I get it," I say. I would have "gotten" whatever she said, but not wanting to go to grad school is an easy base. "I gave up on a few dreams for that same reason."

Rosemary and I talk about everything: our jobs, our school, our family, and a little about our boyfriends. The wine helps to loosen our conversation, but not so much that I give away my secret. I swerved the conversation hard away whenever we got close, but she still told me enough about hers to make me jealous.

I want what they have: love, mutual respect, and a sense of security. She didn't say anything about feeling like she's *too much* or she's the *crazy* one, so that right there is enough to stack above me and Charlie. I swerved, and Rosemary and I have a nice time. We're friends now, and it feels like a light comes on in my dark, dark tunnel of sadness. I feel like I just might get through this.

Friday, December 27

I've been doing a lot of thinking since my appointment with Dr. Miller—mostly the kind of "How did I get this bad?" and "How long has it been going on?" I'm still a little wigged out by the diagnosis, and it's making me reflect on myself a lot. I'm desperately looking for answers I don't think anyone can give. I'm nothing if not an amateur psychiatrist.

I can think of the first episode in my montage of what I now know is my *mental illness*. I didn't see it for what it was at the time-no one did-but my ADHD diagnosis has cleared some of the fog from my lifetime of difference.

I was in elementary school on the playground when I had what the uninformed call a "breakdown." I don't remember what caused it or what made me so upset, but I do remember standing alone on the blacktop having my first panic attack. Its torment felt a lot like when I was asked to read aloud to the class, except this version was more tangible to everybody around me.

It's like I was paralyzed. I remember standing in the middle of everything, of *everyone,* unable to move because my feet felt like they were melted into the cement below me. I remember wanting to run, to hide, but I couldn't. I had no idea what was happening or how to bring myself out of it, so I just stood there for minutes-felt like hours-until a teacher found me. When she did, I was hyperventilating and sweating through my favorite red shirt. The one with the polka dots.

I told the teacher my chest was hurting, and they rushed me from the middle of the playground to the hospital's emergency room. Truly, I thought I was having a heart attack. My uncle died from a heart attack a couple years earlier, and I heard he had chest pain, so I thought I was just following suit. I guess that teacher wasn't taking any chances, either, because she shuffled me off the playground as soon as the words "chest" and "hurting" came from my tiny lips.

So, I guess elementary school is when everything started. My comprehension of that fact is a lot clearer in hindsight and when I have a diagnosis to use for justification. The things I've always written off as *Madison-isms* and the thoughts I assumed everyone else suffers from, turns out, are just mine. I'm on an island of sorts: me and my disorder.

My sickness only got worse as I got older. I see that now. By the time I hit my second year in high school, I had an unvaried routine of managing my checks, paranoias, and doubts. My habits and obsessions were time-consuming; exhausting, both physically and mentally; and they were getting in the way of my making friends and fitting in at school. The kids from elementary who used to follow me around and mimic my behaviors because I was *cool* grew older and realized I was just *weird*. Being "cool" took a new meaning; where it used to look like my supposed disinterest in schoolwork and an objection to assignments, it matured into passing exam grades and completing homework. All of a sudden I was out of the running, and my peers stepped out of my circle.

I was able to ignore my variance for a few more years because I developed habits to compensate for it. I glided through the remainder of my schooling and landed on my feet, then I was even able to land a full-time administrative job in health insurance. Now, present day, I have not only a diagnosis that shines a floodlight over my years of difference, but I also have what I'm hoping is a fix for my *things*. Or, at least, a little relief.

I don't really know what I believe about all this. Either I have ADHD and that explains my years of contrast, or something else is *wrong with me*. ADHD seems too simple for the complexity of what I deal with every day, but Dr. Miller ran the tests, and the data doesn't lie. Even smart people make mistakes, though, so I might get a second opinion.

This is a lot. I don't really want to be alone in it, but there's also no benefit to worrying anyone else about it. Still, it makes me miss Charlie.

Thursday, January 9

I've done a lot of reflecting since I last wrote here. I've spent the last weeks trying to talk myself into the ADHD diagnosis, I guess, but I still have some doubts. Questions unanswered. It's *denial,* maybe, but I'm calling it doubt.

I'm still following Dr. Miller's instructions, and I've taken my Adderall twice per day for almost a month, but I'm not totally on board yet. I just don't feel any different. The "AHAs" I felt when he diagnosed me are fuzzier and less decisive than they were. In the end, the only thing taking that pill has changed is my mind: I was wrong about having ADHD, something else is going on, and I need more help. I need to see someone better, more specialized, than Dr. Miller.

So, again, I took to the internet. I entered a few of my symptoms to find a doctor for my chaos, I was steered down a rabbit hole of information about psychiatrists, and I landed on an office nearby. The practice website introduced me to Dr. Joan Ferguson, whose headshot shows off her wide and trusting smile. I made an appointment for later that same week.

In person, Dr. Ferguson is everything I hope for and want-*need*-at this point in my mental health episode. She's a tiny, soft-spoken woman, but she's direct. She carries herself with confidence, and she seems well-versed. Consistent with her picture on the website, Dr. Ferguson's smile is her best-selling point: her teeth are white, her smile translates to her eyes, and she carries herself in a way that makes me want to tell her everything I know. The combination of my desperation and her very straight teeth have that effect on me, so at least I'm aware.

I see her on Thursday, and it goes very similarly to my visit with Dr. Miller. She asks me questions about my behaviors; I tell her about some of my obsessions and delusions, and she scribbles on a piece of paper the entire time I talk. Apparently, everything I say walks me straight into a diagnosis. But I talk, and I talk. I tell her *everything.*

When I finish, she looks me square in the eyes and says she has a "hunch"-her word-that I've been misdiagnosed. Relief floods me. Dr. Ferguson is my second shot at some clarity and a proper diagnosis. I wasn't so keen on round two of the guessing game, but this time feels more promising.

Dr. Ferguson glances down at her paper, then up to me with none of the forced compassion that Dr. Miller was coated in.

"You don't have ADHD, Madison," she says with a straight face. She's professional, not sympathetic, and she isn't accounting for any of my supposed embarrassment. I appreciate that. "I believe you have something called obsessive-compulsive disorder, or OCD."

She talks me through what an OCD diagnosis means and gives me a handful of pamphlets to read when I get home, but I'm not a blockhead. I know about OCD. It's just unexpected; I was so sure I had something more *normal* like ADHD, so Dr. Ferguson's claim of OCD catches me off-guard. It seems too exotic, too bougie, to be in my file.

I hear her out, though, and I actually come out the other side *preferring* to have ADHD-it's much more manageable than the alternative. See how my mindset changed? "I wish I had the other mental disorder instead of this one," versus "nothing is wrong with me-I don't need any of this." Denial turned to acceptance.

"People with obsessive-compulsive disorder often suffer from a secondary illness caused by an imbalance of their brain chemicals," she continues. "Your habit of ripping out your eyelashes makes me think you also have something called trichotillomania."

As Dr. Ferguson explains, trichotillomania is an overwhelming urge to pull out your own hair. So, in my case, my eyelashes. Honestly, that word sounds like a word some kid made up. She smiles her pearly teeth after saying it, though, so I don't shut her down right away. She goes on.

"You said you've swallowed your pulled lashes before, and that's also common." I hate how she's grouping me into being one of the *commons* of people with OCD, and I start to hate how the words sound coming out of her mouth. I can feel my denial creeping back in. I wish there was a way I can hide my eyelashes, or lack of them, from her at this moment. Or, better yet, I wish there was a way to run out of there. "The problem with swallowing your hair is it might clump up," she points to my stomach, "and cause a blockage."

I don't like what Dr. Ferguson is saying, her friendly voice, her pointing at my stomach like she is my friend, and her regard for my eyelashes. I just don't like it. I'm not sure if I fully believe what she's saying, either, and that's probably why I've turned on her so fast. It's an overload, and she just happens to be steering the ship. I've seen other people pulling out their eyelashes, and some even pulling chunks of their head hair. I know I'm not the only one who doesn't like to read aloud, and I'm thankful for my awareness of taking care of my body. I thought I was *normal*.

Turns out, Dr. Ferguson says, I do those things a little *too much*. I can hear Charlie's voice in her words. The more things she decides about me, the more similar the appointment feels to the one with Dr. Miller. I hate it.

"The Adderall you're taking might actually be triggering your OCD." She keeps on, despite the thick frown lines across my forehead. But she also has my full attention. "It's a good drug for ADHD because it's a stimulant, so it would reinforce your attention and concentration. But you don't have ADHD, so it's working against what *your* brain needs. It increases your irritability and your focus on your obsessions and compulsions, which was probably making your OCD worse."

I'm listening to her talk-I promise I am-but a lot of it is going over my head. Like a fog of dread floating through, making it difficult to pay attention to or comprehend what she was saying. The irony.

"I'm calling in an SSRI for you to start," she continues. "You'll see it called an antidepressant, but I'm prescribing it because it'll raise serotonin levels and get your brain back on track." She looks up from her clipboard then, which forces my full attention. "Flush those other pills down the toilet."

This appointment will take me a few more days to fully sink in because I'm having a harder time accepting everything she said. She piled on a lot more on me than Dr. Miller had, though, so maybe that makes sense.

I stopped taking Adderall and I pick up the antidepressants, but it takes me a while longer to take them. I use that time to reflect on the *things* I do, the beliefs I have, and the habits I've normalized, which lands me in a place of peace with myself.

Some. I accept that my mind could very well be infected with OCD, but I'm not willing to define myself by it. My obsessions and compulsions can be extreme and near-debilitating, but not *everything* I do has to fall under the category of Proof or Evidence of My Disorder. In almost every area of my life, I live comfortably within my disordered mind. I've had it my whole life, so I've found ways to live blissfully alongside it. Sure, I might get preoccupied with *unnecessary* things, and I might not be able to do things in the *timeliest* manner, but I'm happy this way. I have control over my environment; I'm less likely to make a silly mistake, and I'm not hurting anyone. The symptoms of my disorder aren't unmanageable-just a little tedious. I'm okay with it.

My second diagnosis of OCD did give more "AHAs" for the things that have distracted and suffocated me for so long, so I appreciate its validation. I have a reason for the things I do-the things I *have to* do-instead of my only explanation being that I'm a loony. I feel better about my *extra* in my head, but I realize that I still look like a loon in other people's. Most of the time I don't really care, but for the times I do, I desperately want to fit in. And I want it to be effortless.

My diagnosis gives me some clarity, sure, but my obsessions and compulsions still hold me back from the comfortable, contented life I see in my peers. My thoughts run in a never-ending loop, and giving a name to my monster didn't slow my wheel of burden. I know my compulsions and obsessions are illogical and I hate that I need them, but I *do* and I can't *just stop*. That's how my disorder often feels: I know that what I'm doing or thinking doesn't make sense, but I can't just stop it. I'm trapped, by myself.

Compared to ADHD, OCD is like a stranger in the night. That's just saying that it's more ambiguous, and there's no real way to get rid of it. There's no pill that'll magically make me *normal,* but Dr. Ferguson did suggest a few things to help me manage my symptoms. Meditation. Journaling. Nature. Vitamins. Breathing. Sleep. A therapist.

I already write in a journal, obviously, and I'm trying to incorporate the others. Therapy is the only one I haven't, though, because I can't afford a copay every week. But if it'll help me, I guess I'll eventually try anything. I want to be *normal*, and I'm tired of everything hanging over my head. I don't want to think about my rituals anymore, to be scared of my nonaction causing something bad to happen, or to worry about what'll happen if I lose control. It's incredible that most people don't compete with any of this stuff-by no good act from them, they just don't. I'm not even going to talk about what's *fair,* because none of this is.

I'm taking the news of my disorder one day at a time: one day, one obsession, and one compulsion at a time. A part of me still doesn't believe in my own pathology, not fully, but that could very well be a stage of my denial. That stage is likely what made me wait a few days before taking the first antidepressant pill from Dr. Ferguson, even though

I had confirmation that it would help. I didn't, and I still don't, believe I'm bad enough off to justify it. I don't feel like taking a pill is necessary. I just don't. But I also can't deny there's something about me. Charlie saw it, Dr. Ferguson saw it, and I've normalized it. So now I'm curious, if nothing else, about what *normal* feels like.

Naming my OCD monster gives some relief, even if it gives double the grief. I had justification for the parts of my every day that I thought were just silly and pointless things I do, and for the things Charlie said make me *too much*. I have a disordered mind, and that's reason enough for me. I never felt like I needed a reason for the way I am, but Charlie makes me feel like I need some meat behind my madness.

"Madness."

Dr. Ferguson served me that meat on a platter, so to speak, so I can't sit blindly to it anymore. I can hardly deny treatment for it, either. Not if it's what Charlie wants. He hasn't said that's what he wants, not specifically, but it'll fix some of the parts of me I know drive him crazy.

I imagine my disorder like an infection spreading in my mind-like water flowing through the pipes, leaking into every available crack. When I was younger, I only had a couple of ruminations to fight down. , I guess it took more doing to put my mind at peace. At this point, nearly everything I do has a compulsion attached to it. My compulsions are little things I do to help me cope with the world, so if we look at them that way, maybe they're a good thing. That's how I'm coming at this. I know I should get some help, but it's also not like I'm doing *harm*.

To say "everything I do has a compulsion attached" isn't true, not literally, but there are enough of them to overwhelm me. I don't remember what simplicity feels like. I know how control feels, though, and that's my addiction. My habits-now I call them rituals-are there for me to hold on to the control I do have, albeit waning. I think about my *things* like they're password attempts, trying to unlock my peace:

Your artwork isn't done until all imperfections are gone. A jack o' lantern is artwork.

The paintings on the wall must be straight, or the room looks like dirty trash.

An eyelash is about to fall out. Pull it out before it does.

It's a rat race, meaning endless and self-defeating. And my rituals worked for a long time, but they didn't last. I just couldn't account for everything. Life got complicated, and my workarounds couldn't cover all the holes. Imagine a washcloth over a sprinkler. The habits I adapted were my washcloth, and they held back the water-my chaos-for a while. Eventually, though, the water seeps through and gets on everything. I was replacing those washcloths as quickly as possible, trying to cover up my lack of control, but I couldn't move fast enough.

I started imagining control as a passenger sitting in the back seat of my car, giving advice and making constant comments. Control always had something to say, and I was usually listening. I had no choice-I didn't know how to turn it off. At some point, I started to feel like I was losing my grip on Control, so I knocked my rituals up a notch. To my analogy, I let Control sit shotgun. My rituals were my partners, however intoxicating, at the same time as they were haunting me. I knew they were an intrusion on my lifestyle, but I also saw that they gave me discipline and purpose. I loved them when they were in my background, then I hated them when they kept me from my balance.

Control had a grip, a strong one, on my life. I was able to manage my deviation when I was in school because my life was structured. My friends accommodated me as much as I accommodated myself by saying things like "that's just how Madison is" and "let her do her thing," even if it was inconvenient. They supported me, so I didn't have to confront my quirks. My quirks were just part of who I was. It worked.

Then I went to college. Those years were extra hard, mostly because I was still undiagnosed. College is hard for a lot of people, though, so my difference was only there to make it harder. Moving to campus forced me into a new environment; it forced me to try to blend in, and it forced me to try to make new friends alongside my variance. All from scratch. Making friends in college shares the same struggle as dating apps: if one person doesn't mesh with your personality or your preferences, you move on. There are hundreds more options to choose from. And people kept moving on from me.

College, specifically the first year, was dark, literally and in my head. It seemed like every new friend I met would get close enough to see my "quirkiness," get *weirded out*, and swipe past. On to the next. I spent a lot of those nights in my room, alone, in the dark. At the end of the summer before sophomore year, I decided I wanted to change. To be more *normal* and to blend in better. I didn't want to and couldn't live another year like my freshman year. I planned to come back in the fall as the same Madison, just turned down a few levels. That meant, first, that I had to loosen Control's grip.

That was the first time I tried to turn off the voice in my head that was giving me suggestions of how things "should be." I just wanted to turn it off, to ignore and distract myself away from it. The voices that used to give me *gentle* suggestions, though, they adapted; my voice changed tone, and it manifested into harsh and demonic commands of what I *must* do, or else. I didn't know how to stop my voices, and, really, that's when fear cropped up. I started to see that I'd given Control too much authority over my life, but turning it off wasn't as easy as just deciding to. I couldn't just say *stop*.

But I wanted out. So I had to figure out how to get it.

Losing my Control is a terrifying concept. If I say *goodbye* to Control, I'm also saying *goodbye* to my concept of orderliness, to my internalized habits developed over the majority of my life, and to the sense of peace that I've talked myself into when things aren't how they "should be." It's not that I don't think I can live my life without the Control, per se, but it's not comfortable. A bunch of suffocating and legitimate questions crowd my head when I think about losing it, and that makes me second-guess my efforts.

What if I become apathetic and completely lose my discipline?

What if my brain stops its obsessions and moves to something more dangerous?

What if I relax too much and my life becomes the chaos I've worked so hard to avoid?

When I so much as think I might want to address my disordered thinking and face my disability head-on, fear of the unpredictability and lack of Control stop me in my tracks. In the end, it makes the most sense to keep taking that pill and ease myself out of my disordered habits, instead of facing them on my own, all at once. I haven't given up on healing myself my way, though, and as naturally as possible. So I've taken stock of my *things* to make sure I can accommodate them all from the driver's seat.

I intend to fix myself. The things Dr. Ferguson said at our appointment made sense, but she's also a *doctor,* so of course, her first answer is to medicate me. But I'm better than that. I can do this my way. I'll take the antidepressant's help, so long as I'm the one behind the wheel.

Control wants me, and the feeling is mutual. It taps on my brain and sends me messages, and it woos me with promises of its security. For the most part, I can resist, but I've accepted that I need to give in sometimes too. It's a balancing act, and I'm figuring out how to make it a healthy one. I've always been a natural-leaning person, so this diagnosis is only giving me a chance to flex those muscles. I'm trying to fix myself, and I'm figuring it out as I go.

Okay. My hand is tired from writing and I don't know what else to say. Or how I should even feel right now. All this time I'm spending by myself is starting to mess with my head.

Fatimah

I'm skinny, and in a lot of ways, it makes my life easier. I'm thin, so I'm respected. That makes perfect sense to me.

My lines are fine, my ink is consistent, and my body is a long, cast-like tube filled with black. I'm wrapped in smooth plastic from tip to end, even in the place a rubber grip would be. I don't slide around when someone holds me, though, not like you'd think. On the contrary, I'm steady and effortless. My plastic casing means I don't cause cramps when I'm used for an extended time, which she often does. My black dries instantly, my nib slides with little pressure, and I wear a cap on my head that clicks in place.

It might sound like I'm bragging, but those are just the facts. I'm a high-quality ink pen for classical writing and drawing, not just a *giveaway* kind. And my name is Fatimah.

I wasn't made for the basic stuff like jotting notes or mindless doodling, but for the important, more dignified script. My ink isn't unlimited, and by the feel of it, it's also not cheap. I'm pulled when she uses her neat handwriting or makes mindful illustrations. Any script outside of that, in my opinion, is a waste. I'll even use the word "offensive."

I'm built differently, better, than an average pen. I just am.

There are other pens out there just like me, of course, but I'm the only size 0.5 in this case. She keeps us all for different reasons. The 0.8, a bigger kid named Bill, is for important messages written in bold letters; Kelly, a size 0.005, is for very skinny lines, adding precise details, and writing in the margins; Pat, the 0.1, is closer to the size of a basic pen, and he's used for simple text; and Kim, the size 1.0, is for loud messages and capital letters. There are a few others, but those I named, including me, are the VIPs. She uses the lot of us most often because we're all-inclusive.

In the middle of the pack, at a perfect size of 0.5, I can do it all. With some pressure, I make a statement, and less pressure makes me slight. My size in the middle means I'm a pen for everything and everybody. A People's Pen. I have range, and I think she recognizes that. I notice she pulls me more than the others. I get it.

Again, it sounds like I'm bragging. But it's just the facts.

All the sizes are here together, in this box. Despite our broad range, we're stuck with each other in this rigid, brown container that snaps out the light. The box keeps us separate from the average, doodle-type pens, which I appreciate. Those pens are just on a different level than we are. That's not me speaking ill of or looking down on—they can't help how they were made—but it wouldn't feel right to lie against or underneath one. That's like putting an apple in a bowl of oranges. The apples, we ink pens, taste heaps better than oranges, the ballpoints. The two just don't mix. See what I'm saying?

It's dark and warm in the container we're stored in, which makes the others happy. I think they like it because it's quiet and they can relax from doing any work, but I think it's boring. I would rather be in the light, writing things, than lying about in the shadows. I think they're also kind of boring. *Lazy.*

The work I do when I'm out of this box is organized, inoffensive, and respectful. When she writes with me, her handwriting is legible and clean. And if it's not, we start over. When I'm drawing pictures, there are always pencil lines on the page for me to trace, so there's less chance for me to make an error. Sometimes she makes pencil lines to trace the letters of her words, too, but that's less common.

Her attentiveness and precision are key to how I've always imagined being used, even before she bought me. I've always just felt that's how it *should be.* I hold myself to a high standard, as I should, and I deserve respect.

In fact, I demand it.

If you've ever had a pen sputter or stop writing despite having enough ink, you've seen what our revenge looks like. Tit for tat.

I'm the one who's *writing* everything the girl puts in her journal, so it would make sense that I *comprehend* everything that's going on in her life—at least the stuff she accounts for. That's a perk of my job. Or not so much. It can be way less fun than it sounds. These days, she mostly writes about someone called *Charlie* and how she's *down* on some things about him. Sometimes it's hard to keep straight, mostly because it's just not very interesting. I used to get a bigger picture of her world, but since he came into the picture, he's mostly all she writes about. Or maybe that's really all that's happening in her world: *Charlie*. She's boring now, as if she's lost her edge.

I used to pay more attention to what she was writing, but I got lost in it. One day, she'd pull me out to write a bunch of happy, positive things in her journal. Those entries were nice, but they were fleeting; her happiness would never hold. The very next entry, sometimes made the very same day, was my gamble: would she be happy, or would it be dark? It was hard to keep up. When her darkness started to become more commonplace, that's when I could see her psyche sliding downhill. Through her writing, I noticed that she was starting to see herself through Charlie's eyes, which are clouded. A *gunky* cloud. Sometimes, when the darkness took over, she wrote about her unhappiness, her anger with him, and her plans to "take care of it." I assumed that meant taking care of her grief around it all, but I don't really know. That's the stuff I couldn't follow.

Adding Charlie to her life, in my diagnosis, has made her second-guess and lose confidence in herself. So, you can imagine, it's a hard thing to have a front-row seat. I took a step back, but only figuratively. Remember, I'm her favorite. But I have stopped caring so much about the words she writes, and I've turned my focus to the bigger picture: managing my ink's output so it doesn't clot and bleed through the paper, maintaining a consistent stream without breaks, and working to preserve my integrity. I fill my mind with all the logistics, and I don't leave space for her world. I can't, not really. At this point, she might be happy or sad—I don't know, and it doesn't matter. She's going to use me to write about it either way, so what do I care? As long as I'm not trapped up in that box, just *lying there* on top of the others, and I'm doing my job, I can justify a wall around myself that keeps her on the outside. It's meant to be for my protection, maybe, but also for her benefit. It's better if I just focus and cut out all the extra.

Still, on some level, I'm aware of everything that goes on around me and everything she's going through because she journals about it. I don't know if she realizes I'm paying attention. If she did, it seems like she'd hold back writing some of the things she does. Or she's confident enough to not care, but I don't think that's it. I don't think she realizes that I'm Wide Awake.

I've been around for a while, so my ink is probably almost gone. All I can do is assume that part, though, because there's no way for me to check. As my luck goes, I'll run out of ink right now, when I finally get a stage to introduce myself. Or maybe I have enough to carry this out longer—who knows? There's really no telling when I'll go so until I do, it's business as usual. I try not to think about all that too much—when my ink runs dry—because there's nothing I can do about it and no way for me to have a clue. But it's just not an easy thing to ignore.

Still, here's me trying.

My name is Fatimah, and I'm a pen. But I'm not just any pen. My tip is a skinny size 0.5, my ink is water-based and smooth, and I'm black. Pens of my like are sold all around the world, but I'm kept in a box on a table, waiting for her next entry. I'm exactly where I want to be. The last time I came out, she used me to draw circles on a pumpkin. But that's not my normal task. Actually, I don't know what that was. It wasn't writing about her feeling *down* about *Charlie*, though, so I'm not complaining.

My work on the ball is where you could maybe call me an artist, but the creativity wasn't mine. It never is. I just trace her lines. I also write poetry sometimes, but most of my work is contained within her journal entries. I guess that's fine. I prefer the times she takes me outside those journal pages because I get to put her personality on a stage and give her thoughts a voice instead of sealing them between the pages. I think she has a lot to offer—if only she would get out there. But there's nothing I can do about that.

Regardless of what she's writing and on which surface, I love what I do. In some way, I love every part of this journey. I don't understand how the others could prefer lying in the box to being out here working. My job as a pen is a *privilege,* the highest privilege, and I love it. But I'm not taking anything for granted.

Journal entries, pencil tracing, and illustrations are the only work I've known, so I have no clue what I'll do when

I run out of ink. Kelly, the size 0.005 with whom I share the box, told me our girl could refill our casts once we run out of ink, but that seems like a lot to hope for. Regardless of my universality and my very high enthusiasm, I know I'm replaceable. There are other 0.5s out there that can pick up where I leave off. It's a bit stressful, making the most of whatever time I still have, but I try to not think about it very much. I just hope I'll be around for a lot longer because I have a lot of things I

Friday, January 17

I drink a lot of tea these days, but mostly because it's part of my routine. And I guess I like it too. I like it okay, but I've really buckled down on it since I read that caffeine might help with some symptoms of my disorder. But I haven't seen much difference. Yet? Perhaps drinking coffee would be a better way to gauge caffeine's benefits, but I'm not about that. I drink two to three cups of tea a day because it's my habit and I enjoy the taste, but my reasoning is just for those. As for my using caffeine to manage my OCD, I've lost some enthusiasm. Caffeine might still be an answer, but I'm throwing some other options in the mix, too. Like keeping this journal.

I started writing down my *things* after Charlie and I first got together, but my reasoning back then was different. Back then, I wanted to remember what it felt like to be happy, and I was seeing myself differently-happier-in the light of my and Charlie's relationship. I used my writing to process the new emotions that were coming at me at full speed: mostly good, some confusing, and only rarely bad. Then, when I got my diagnosis and-you know this-Charlie wasn't the only thing that sat in my mind. This journal became a place for me to not only pick apart my relationship, but to better understand who and how I am. Writing here has helped me become more aware of myself, my thoughts, and my processes.

Keyword: *Awareness*.

I think that'll be my ticket away from my disorder. If I can be aware of what I'm doing and of my destructive thinking, I can just stop it. Right? I'm counting on my cure as being as simple as *just stop it*.

I might not be as mentally strong as that yet, but I'm working on it. The combination of my caffeine intake and some self-awareness ought to give me more Control over my disorder than any medicine can. I'm sure of it.

That's why I've decided to stop taking the antidepressant Dr. Ferguson prescribed.

They were making me tired, my stomach sometimes upset, and feeling sluggy. I didn't see a difference in my obsessive thinking, either. I'm going back to healing *my* way. The natural way.

Dropping those pills and taking back the metaphorical steering wheel means I really have to kick up my awareness of everything going on in my body. Writing in this journal has helped; I've been better at recognizing my triggers and understanding the anxieties that get me to my rituals, and sometimes I can stop myself from going through with them. When I met with Dr. Ferguson, she suggested journaling "to help *soften* the symptoms of" my disorder. I didn't tell her I already keep a journal to write about my ex-boyfriend, though. *Haha!* Because I don't think that's what she meant. *Joan* doesn't look like someone who can relate to my broken heart. With her confidence and intelligence, I wouldn't be surprised if she always has the upper hand in her relationships. Like a superhero or something.

Dr. Ferguson told me to use this journal to write down my beliefs and triggers, then "challenge them to identify the real versus imagined." Okay, but that sounds useless. Maybe this is just my version of her suggestion: lots about

Charlie, a little about how I'm healing, and even less about my disordered practices. Once again, I'm only going half-way. We'll see how it works.

Tuesday, January 31

As good as I am about keeping habits, I'm trying to make a habit of writing down my *things* in here instead of accommodating them without thinking much about them. For a little while, I carried around a pocket-sized version of this notebook so I could always have it for rescue when my mind tells me, *Pull on your eyelashes* or *brush your teeth for one minute longer*. I'm trying to be good so that I can justify going against what Dr. Ferguson prescribed. But it's a lot to keep track of: caffeine, meditation, caffeine again, vitamins, serotonin, and journaling throughout. I'm pretty good about eating healthy and drinking caffeine, but some habits are harder to adopt.

Anyway, journaling feels useless. And maybe that's why I forget about it so easily. Counting out my beliefs and addictions on paper doesn't do anything in the way of getting me to stop them. If I didn't think my behaviors were realistic, I wouldn't have them. I'm not stupid.

If I wasn't scared of getting toxic shock syndrome from leaving my tampon in too long, I wouldn't change it as often as I do.

If I believed my body wouldn't be poisoned by expired food that the FDA somehow deems "safe" for consumers, I wouldn't be so uptight about throwing it away the moment it expires.

If I wasn't worried about brushing my gums off, I would brush my teeth five times a day instead of two.

Seeing a version of my compulsions written out on paper doesn't do anything to make them less crippling. Actually, writing them out and reading them back makes me feel crazier. I know my fears can be unreasonable and my superstitions often mean nothing, but at the same time, they mean everything. I can't stop them, and I'm not even sure if I want to. I can't imagine not following those thoughts, whatever pops into my head.

Writing out my *things* makes me focus on them too much, then they feel worse. I need something that will take me away from my thoughts, not put my focus on them. That's why I've decided to use this journal more for my relationship crisis than for my mental one. As much as it *doesn't* help my disordered mind, it *does* help my processing the Charlie situation.

That doesn't mean I've given up on my healing, though. Not at all. I tried something new last week that I read about on the internet. Chewing gum. I read that the motion of chewing will reduce my cortisol levels when I get stressed, making me less likely to obsess and compulse. I figured I can just as easily pop a piece in my mouth when I'm tempted to "be OCD." I have nothing to lose, or I thought.

I chewed more gum than I have in my life for two whole days-until I saw myself walking past a store's mirror: I looked like a horse chomping on grass. And that was my last piece. I stopped, for vanity.

So, here I am, giving this a second shot. After three-ish weeks of being away from it, I looked back on some old entries and tried to read my compulsions like a story, instead of my personal account.

Objectivity is today's word.

From reading my entries, I see the power I've given my disorder over my mind and my behavior. A few things really jump out at me and make it clear how improbable my obsessions have gotten. It's embarrassing, almost.

I'm back in these pages, but please know I'm rolling my eyes hard because it's a big "told ya so" moment for Dr. Ferguson. I'll never admit it to her, though. No way. Call this my round two of journaling and, this time, I hope all my awareness will bring that *improbable* mindset into the moment of my compulsions. That's what the internet said will happen. Round two, and I'm gonna try to focus less on Charlie and more on me. My mind.

Besides, there's not much to write about Charlie aside from: STILL NOTHING. STILL SAD. Charlie and I are off of Cloud Nine, and we're still fighting. There isn't much else to say about it.

I've been thinking a lot since my diagnosis. About myself, my driving forces, and my everyday. I recognize how much my OCD interferes with my life; from the moment I wake up and eat breakfast until I turn off the lights for bed, I'm ritualizing. I'd stopped thinking about all the extra *things* I do because I've done them for so long, but now I see how much my obsessions and compulsions are time sucks. It's good and *normal* that I'd become blind to my everyday patterns-necessary or not-but it just made diagnosing my variance that much trickier.

I *have* been diagnosed, and I'm trying to heal my mind the right way. I started a few new habits (drinking caffeine, journaling, meditating) when I thought I had ADHD, but my fortune, the research for a DIY ADHD fix is nearly parallel to OCD's. That's fewer new habits for me to adopt, and it makes my compliance easier. *Onward.*

I'm doing it right this time because I want to get better. I'm going to write in a journal every day, no matter how insignificant it feels. If it's just a few sentences *("I woke up in a good mood and got a lot done today.")* or a few paragraphs *("Charlie and I had an argument over something stupid last night, and I'm still thinking about it. It feels like his patience is running out . . .")*, I'm going to make that effort. I know my tendency to justify myself out of things I don't want to do, so I'm going to make it a habit I can look forward to. I'll sit at my desk by the window with my afternoon cup of tea, light a candle to help me relax, and write in my best handwriting with a new set of pens, in a brand-new notebook. There's something about the mood of a lit candle and a new set of office supplies to get me excited about self-care.

I've reached the stage in life where self-care can be as dull as writing about my manias and fights with my boyfriend in a letter to myself. I'm also at the stage where I'm excited about it, mostly because I treated myself to a new pack of ink pens. Kid Madison would be rolling her eyes the hardest.

I've referred to our fights and his lack of patience, but Charlie and I can get back to that good place. I know we can. And once we're back together and happy, the downs of our roller coaster will feel worth it. Before this last fight we had, we were an ordinary couple that fought about *ordinary* stuff. I think. He has his own apartment, and he's not here

100 percent of the time, so that helps. He comes around enough to offset my loneliness, but irregularly enough to give us both space when we need it. I like when he's around, but the balance is nice. I don't know if I'd feel the same way if he was here all the time, living with me. That would be too much for both of us.

I miss when Charlie and I were happy and when he came around here, but I can also feel my sadness turning into apathy. That might be what "getting over him" feels like. So I guess it's a good thing?

Thursday, February 6

Even though we're not talking right now, Charlie still keeps some of his things here: a toothbrush, an extra t-shirt, a bar of soap. His stuff is still here either because he doesn't want to see me long enough to pick them back up or because there's a glimmer of hope that we'll get back together again. I prefer and I hang onto the latter.

When we're On, Charlie stays the night sometimes. Most of the time, though, I prefer sleeping in the apartment by myself. His occasional overnight company was a fairly new step for us-he would never be able to sleep over when I was at my parents' house. And it was nice, I'll admit. There's another perk of my living alone.

Every time we fight and "break up" (I think that's what this is), it feels like we take a giant step backward. I don't know. Living alongside his things in our Off times is kinda hard, but I think I'd prefer it to the finality of him taking them away. Still, though, I move his stuff around so I don't have to look at it day in and day out. Especially now, living alongside all of Charlie's junk makes me sad and a little aggravated.

My feelings are all over the place. I guess that's not a surprise.

I've never had a boyfriend as an adult before, never anyone to acknowledge me outside the school's hallways and lunchroom. So a lot of how I act with Charlie is on-the-fly. I'm not as pathetic as I sound, I don't think. Charlie doesn't actually know how inexperienced I am at being in a relationship, either, and I'm trying to keep it that way. That's why all this writing and processing I'm doing has helped with sorting my emotions.

I'm falling into some routines since I moved out of my parents', journaling is only the first, and that makes me feel more *adult*. Because that's what adults do, right? They-we-keep routines. The repetition and schedule of it all make living alone feel less like I'm play-acting and more like I might have my adult-sized ducks in a row. The silence of my solitude, like I said, was the first wake-up call after moving out, and that didn't come easy at first. But then came the freedom: to play my music loud, to walk around in my panties, and to drown my thoughts with the voice of an unnecessarily loud podcast host. I love when Charlie is here and I love having him to talk to, but the contrast of my freedom is also nice. That freedom is giving my mind time and space to heal.

I'm doing the work to fix myself, even if it feels useless sometimes. I want my mind to heal, and I want to fit in with the people around me. I want to get better on my own terms so that just means I have to do a bit more than I was prescribed. That's a whole extra workload I'm putting on myself, but if there's success, it'll be worth it. I've done some research on cognitive-behavioral therapy, the kind Dr. Ferguson recommended for my OCD, and I'm even trying to incorporate some of its principles into my routine.

When I feel anxiety around an object or experience, I'll acknowledge it, evaluate its validity then, if possible, remove it.

If I can't get away from the anxiety-inducing stimulus, I won't avoid it but try to relax my mind in its midst.

I trust myself to handle difficult situations. I'm no different from them. I can handle whatever comes at me.

Some of my obsessions are excessive. I know that. There's a foundation of validity in all of them, though, or I would be able to drop them way easier. The feelings I have that lead to my compulsions are also valid. You can't convince me that my feelings aren't real. The compulsions attached are completely manageable for me—at least at this point. But I'm just not *normal*. You see my problem? I can live alongside this disorder—I have for a long time. All my work to get rid of it is like extra credit. It's the work I didn't realize I needed to do until it was pointed out so sharply to me. By Charlie, you can guess.

Obsessive-compulsive disorder is physiological, and my diagnosis is *not my fault*. It doesn't determine anything about my character or my worth, but it sure does get in the way. It's just for that reason that I want it gone.

Margaret

My name is Margaret, but you can call me Marge. You're the only one calling me anything, really, so I'd like to keep it simple. Marge is easier to remember, and I want you to remember me for a while. I don't know how much longer I'll be around.

I get smaller and slighter with each passing day until eventually, I'll be gone. I think that's coming pretty soon. The wax of my body is a shadowed orange and my jar calls me Pumpkin Pie, but I'm not as indulged as I'd like to be. In fact, I feel a lot closer to soap—the cheap, bar kind that you get at a hotel for free. I identify easier with that: smells a little bit like dirt, leaves a slimy film on your surface, and flakes apart after a couple of uses. I have three strings coming out of my top, so that means I'm not *actually* cheap. I just smell like it.

There's somebody for everybody, I guess, because my strings are constantly burnin'. She must love the smell of dirt and cheap soap. I'm a candle, but I guess you figured out that much.

I could be proud of being lit so often and nearly used up, but I'm not. My wax is almost to the bottom of my jar; my strings are tall and blackened, and I'm far from content. I've melted down way quicker than I anticipated, and I don't like myself very much. My smell. I'm not confident, so I'm not happy. And that's just it.

There are a few great things about being a candle that make the bad parts worth it—the greatest being the time I spend burning. I'm not saying I take any pleasure in the initial lighting and certain shock of being set on fire because that part never gets easier. The "great" happens after I've burned enough for the flame to numb my senses, when my surroundings become a blur, and when that calm has settled in.

There are some things I have to get through before I reach that bliss, though, and every one of them is a sacrifice.

Our routine is this: she picks me out, usually first, from a row of two other candles sitting nearby on this table, then she'll pull me close to her face. She holds me there—still and close—for a few more seconds. There are sometimes tears in her eyes, and she sometimes hovers close for longer than she does with others. I'm not sure what all that means, but it feels genuine. Those moments feel like they're ours. I'm not exactly sure what kind of moments they are, but that's more than the other candles can say.

I'm holding on to a fantasy that one day she'll whisper something like, "You're my favorite, Marge" or "I love you,

Margaret" while holding me inches away. That part hasn't happened yet, but the water in her eyes and the smile that follows her deep inhale when I'm close is good enough for now. She doesn't have to say those words yet. I know she feels them. Still, though, I fantasize.

Those seconds are always my last peaceful ones for a while. I'll call them the last calm flashes before my *firestorm*. Before my commotion begins.

I've lived this over and over. Her smile and inhale are, truly, my last moments of rest. The peace before a pandemic. The smoke before a house fire. Those moments are pure and sweet, like a newborn baby can be. Then, the baby grows up to be Hitler.

Click, click, click, poomph.

The *poomph*—my mark. My trigger. All good feelings are gone, and I'm on fire.

I have about three seconds before the *storm* touches down. Put differently, I have three seconds before I'm on fire and in certain pain. The fire bites at my strings first, so I'm thankful to have three up there for buffer. Those strings take away the shock of it all, and they give me another second of quiet before I have to feel the pain of anything. They could also be why I go through all this suffering to begin with, though. If they weren't up there, maybe I would get to just relax. I don't know. I guess it doesn't matter much, though, because they're there and I do.

Three strings up top *do* make me feel more bougie, but I'd be okay with none at all. No strings would mean I'm a darkened orange block of wax for display, Maybe shaped like a dog or a pair of legs. It's not worth thinking about too much, though, because those strings are stuck deep in me for as long as I'm around. They're not going anywhere; we're a package deal, me and the three. I try not to be resentful.

The *poomph*, then *1. . . 2 . . . 3 . . .*

The flame travels down all three strings until it reaches my top. It takes another few seconds for the burning, biting pain from the fire to register with me—I call that my shock. Once the burn starts, though, giddy up. It's quick to spread, and it's all-encompassing.

This part, I imagine, would be the same feeling as all of your body parts burning in a fire. The equivalence would mean you'd have to burn your body every afternoon for hours at a time, though, so maybe that doesn't hit the target. I don't really know how to compare it.

My burning pain turns to a halfway numb, but still passionate, itch all over my body. These are the itches that can't be scratched. Especially in my case because they're centralized to where the fire touches my wax's surface. When it happens, my wax starts to melt into a swimming pool on the surface, and the itching gets so intense and mindful that it's hard not to lose focus on everything else, including my pain. I'm a weird, sad kind of thankful for the itchy part. Still, though, it's horrific.

The itchiness lasts about a minute before it stops suddenly, and fatigue takes its place. The fatigue comes fast and hard, and this is where I go fully numb. My top wax hosts the swimming pool, and the callosity of it lets me relax. In my numbness, I get some of those good feelings back. The dulling of my sensations puts my pain and irritation back into my background, and I slide into a sleepy peace. Recently, as I've melted down shorter and my strings are longer with more callous, that sleepy peace comes a little quicker.

This is the first opportunity I've had to share my narrative, and I've been excited about it for a while. But I don't want my enthusiasm to push my story along too fast. There's more to me and my job than the suffering. I'm not *always* lit.

I sit on a table with a few other candles that burn alongside me. Kind of like my strings are part of my package, I'm a package deal with them. We always get lit together. None of us are the same, though, so that keeps it interesting. Mildly. We're a pretty random mix: one smells like a nut, the other smells like baby powder, and I smell like dirty hotel soap. I don't see how we make a good combination, but she seems to like us together, so here we are. Together, always.

It seems like we'd be good, cozy friends by now, but I don't even know their names. It's fine.

The three of us, the *amigos*, are set in a row on her desk. I think. Whatever this surface is, she visits it about once a day to fire us up and hang out for a bit. It's nice to have her nearby while I agonize, then to keep me company when I'm numb and resting. The other candles are fine company, too, but it's not the same as having her. I don't know. The three of us have so much in common, but I still prefer her.

I like it when she's here and I'm glad for my numb peace, but I get a tiny bit shorter every time she burns me. I don't know what'll happen when I shrink to my bottom, but I guess I'm on my way to finding out. *Slowly,* but I'm getting there. Once I melt away completely, I think I'll be gone for good. I don't suppose there's any coming back from that. I also don't know if it's going to hurt. My Catch-22 is that I like when she chooses me and when I reach the peace, but I get closer to my end with every swimming pool I make. The closer I get, the more exposed I am and the more aware I am of everything around me. My wax melting is some version of an expiration, and I don't feel ready for it. It's happening, though. I just hope it won't hurt. I don't know *how* or even *if* I can handle any more pain.

You understand that there are some good parts of this, being a candle, but at a premium. Showing up as a pair of waxed legs is appealing in a lot of ways, except that I'm not entirely willing to give up some parts of my vocation. Specifically, her attention and the numb ending after each burn. Even the burning, as uncomfortable and painful as it is, is *something.* Sitting on this desk as a pair of legs, while seductive and particularly undeniable, would mean I wouldn't feel anything. Ever. No pain, no numbness, nothing. It's nice when I reach my sleepy peace, but there needs to be a balance. I need a better way of getting there.

Also, it's not like I can just choose to be a sculpture. I'm part of a package, remember?

I'll be gone soon, and I'm pretty sure I won't be back. I hope I'll at least leave behind the memory of my dirty scent, and I hope my light will shine for a bit afterward—if only in her recollection.

But I'm just a candle. I'm replaceable, I know that. I've burned hot; I've overcome a lot of my agony, and I've smelled like dirt the whole time. But I'm good for her, at least for now, because she's burnin' me up fast.

My name is Margaret, Marge, and some bits of me will last forever. Perhaps in a lingering smell, in her fond memories, or in the orange dot of my wax that spilled from my swimming pool to her desk this afternoon.

Tuesday, February 11

"Hey, Madison." Charlie's voice sings through the phone. My heart leaps, then it sinks again. Old habits.

"Oh," I say. He's the last person I expected to hear from. "Hi, Charlie."

"How are you?" he asks. His voice sounds softer than I've ever heard it. Because he misses me, I hope.

"I'm okay, Charlie," I say. Spending time with Rosemary and her boyfriend dragged Charlie off his pedestal, then down a few levels. He's not as great as I once thought-I see that now. "Can I help you?"

"I was just seeing how you're doing," he says.

"I'm great," I answer, maybe too quickly. Calling to "*see how I'm doing*" makes me feel like a sick patient. Or like he's my brother checking in on me. I might have struggled with living alone at first, but I'm fine now. I have one friend, and I made her by *myself*. You can't tell me I'm not doing great. "How are you?"

"I wanted to see if you wanna try to meet up again," he says. Like it wasn't entirely his fault it didn't work the first time. "Maybe for coffee or something."

"That would be nice," I say. The ice in my voice is starting to melt. It feels good to have some power back. I'm not sitting in the driver's seat yet, not totally, but I'm at least on the center console with one butt cheek touching the seat. "I have plans on Saturday morning, but maybe in the afternoon?"

A half lie. I'll call Rosemary and *make plans* for Saturday morning. To *get ready* for the afternoon. Further, Charlie needs to know he's not my priority anymore.

"Okay." He sounds shocked, or is it just my imagination? "How about that place on Moreland Street at 2 p.m.?"

"I'll see you then," I say and hang up the phone without saying "bye." Rosemary taught me that.

Wednesday, February 12

"What are your plans on Saturday morning?" I start talking as soon as I hear the *click* of an answered phone.

"Hello to you too," Rosemary says. I can hear her smiling through the sass. "I don't have anything. What's up?"

"I need you to help me look hot," I say. I sat on Charlie's invitation for a while-only a day-to figure out how I feel about it. The feeling I came to was "why not hear him out?" but also, "I'm going to need help." I decided if I was going to show up, I needed to look good. *Really* good. To show him what he's missing.

And I'll need some help.

"I'm meeting Charlie for coffee on Saturday. I need to-" She doesn't know Charlie and I are on a break. *Careful now.* "I wanna look good," I finish.

"My specialty," she says. "I'll bring my makeup and a dress I just bought. It's gorgeous." She pauses, and I hear her shuffling things around in the background. "I have a few tops that'll look good on you too."

"Perfect," I say. Makeup because I don't have any and a borrowed outfit because I haven't bought anything new since I moved in here. Showing up in something Charlie hasn't seen will maybe show him that my life is moving on fine without him. Or, if not, it'll just make me feel cuter. "See you then."

And she hangs up.

Sunday, February 16

My coffee date with Charlie was fine, I guess. I don't know if I should call it a "date," but whatever it was, it was kinda weird. Rosemary came over in the morning to help me get ready, and she made me look better than I thought I could.

I wore her "gorgeous" dress that actually looked nice on me; she used the still-new mascara I bought when Charlie canceled on me the first time; and she painted my face with more brushes and wands than I could keep track of.

I felt good about myself. But Charlie didn't seem to notice.

He forgot that I don't drink coffee, then was offended when I reminded him. I ordered a hot tea that didn't cool down enough to drink before he had to leave, so I just pitched it. Everything about it was disappointing. He talked about himself the whole time, catching me up on things that have happened to him since we last talked. *Like I care.* He didn't say anything in the way of regretting how horribly he treated me or about how I've been since our last blowup, but he had lots to say about his roommates, how much he likes his new gym, and how tired he feels around 9:30 every night. I listened to it all, though, and I looked good doing it. *Hot. What a waste.*

Saturday, February 22

Even with the good things happening to me lately, my mental health has been dragging me down. Like a wet blanket I'm pulling behind me across the pavement. That's not my being melodramatic as much as a response to all the changes in my life these past six months. I've never had to lend my mental health so much of my consideration, so it has exhausted just as much as confused me. Some days I'm functioning normally and everything is easy, then some days I feel like the wind was knocked out of me. The latter usually happens when I'm alone and in my head for too long.

I'm going through some of the motions Dr. Ferguson prescribed with my diagnosis, and I'm incorporating some I researched on the internet. I need to come at this disorder from all angles, I've decided, if I want to fix myself. Dr. Ferguson's ideas came from a place of helping me "supplement and strengthen your SSRI prescription," and the internet works in the classroom of "healing yourself without mediation." My happy medium: I've filled my prescription, but I save the pills for my bad days, the days I'm feeling particularly down. That's the halfway point. Where I would like to go cold turkey from all medication, I keep the antidepressants nearby. Just in case. Every day, though, I keep a schedule of activity, wellness, and health-forward habits so I won't get to that point. In practice, that just looks like a pill bottle sitting next to my sink, untouched. My bad days never feel *bad* enough.

I'm meeting this diagnosis halfway, to see what I can do.

I took a Clinical Psychology class in college that taught me how versatile our brains can be; with lots of dedication and the right approach, we can manipulate them into and out of almost any situation. The antidepressant, Dr. Ferguson said, will take about six weeks to show its full effect. That window of waiting gives me time to adopt and test the effectiveness of my own habits before the drug's serotonin boost takes over. The six-week timeline is for people who take the pills consistently, too, which I don't plan on doing. So I might have a bigger window to work in.

I've never had an opportunity to manipulate and test my brain before, not until I landed this diagnosis. In a way, the time and money I put into my education paved the road for managing my OCD diagnosis later in life. There's more of my justification.

I think writing everything here, in this journal, has helped a lot. It feels like a best friend I can tell everything to without feeling judged. I don't have one of those yet. I'm getting there with Rosemary, but I'm still chin-deep in some of the lies I've told. I look forward to when I can be honest about everything, but I need Charlie back before I can do that. I wish I could be vulnerable with him, too, but we haven't gotten there yet. He used to do this thing where he'd fake-snore and pretend to fall asleep when I tell stories-I think as a joke that I talk too much or I'm not being interesting enough. He would claim he's *kidding* and it's all a *joke,* but I think it has some big-picture truth too. Charlie isn't interested in what I say; I don't feel safe totally opening up to him, and I'm better off not talking at all. I'm over-aware of what I tell him now, and I don't talk about things that don't have to do with him; if it doesn't directly affect him, I feel like he just doesn't care about what I have to say. It's okay. We'll get there.

Part of the advice from Dr. Ferguson was to journal-which I'm doing-but I'm trying to make it something I look forward to. My attempt: light candles. To set the mood, I guess? The introspection it takes to sit down and write about myself is the exact opposite of what I'm comfortable with, so I'm trying to do things that'll get me excited about the process. I bought a new box of Fine Line pens; I'm using a separate, still fairly new notebook; and I time my journaling sessions with my afternoon cup of tea. It's becoming a part of my day I look forward to, and it's my chance to dump all the things floating around my head onto a piece of paper.

Especially stuff about Charlie. Writing it all out forces me to dump it, step away from it, then come back from a different perspective. I'm fighting hard for him, so there's a lot to get out. I'm fighting *for* him, finally, not *with* him. There's a lot in my writing about the *with*, though, because those times leave a dent.

I compare my and Charlie's relationship to Rosemary and her boyfriend's a lot: how they talk to each other, how neither of them seems to lose patience with the other, and how she talks about their collaboration. I've always wanted that in Charlie-a teammate, not an opponent. But I'm not perfect, so I can't expect him to be. He'll come back to me eventually, and we'll work on it. We can be better.

The overlapping of my new habits-drinking tea, keeping a journal, lighting my candles-keeps me on track with who I want to be. Overlapping them makes it easier because I can get them all out of the way in one go. Dr. Ferguson suggested I also try meditation to manage my triggers, and I gave it a solid try. I did. Maybe I wasn't doing something right, but I kept falling asleep when I lay on the floor and tried to *experience my body* and *feel my breath leaving my lungs*. I know about active meditation and achieving calmness through movement, and I figure my hand moving across this page is movement enough. Two birds, one stone.

I've also read some about using aromatherapy to induce a relaxing, meditation-like mood. That's where the candles fit in the puzzle. But I also just like messing with fire. One stone, and we're gettin' all the birds.

I have three candles in rotation right now: Pumpkin Pie, my favorite; Chestnut Macchiato; and Vanilla Soy. I got those last two on mega discount so they don't smell like much, but I burn them anyway. For ambiance. Pie is the star of the show, so that's where I dropped the most money. I picked it because it reminds me of Charlie, of the time we went to the pumpkin patch, of what I thought was our budding love, and of the Good Times. I never thought I was the type to romanticize an inanimate object-a *candle*, no less-but here I am. I've even cried sitting with that candle before. That happened in the beginning when I was freshly single, freshly alone, and before I saw a flicker of hope in getting him back. I'm not usually that sentimental, but I was heartbroken. I still kinda am.

Sitting with the candle's pumpkin scent and my remembering the Good Times with Charlie are both healthy, I think, but also hard. I'm not sure if sitting in those memories is helping me get over him, but I'm also not willing *not* to. Getting over someone feels so final, and I'm still a little raw from all this. From our last argument. He said some things about me that stung a little bit because they might be true: I might be *crazy*, and I might be a *waste of his time*. He chipped my confidence so low that I'm not even sure I can fault him for his words anymore. Charlie might be right, and it may have been a kindness to tell me those things about myself. Sure, his delivery and his vicious expression were not kindnesses, but there was some meat behind his brute.

I think my rituals are helping heal me, so I think I'm on the right track. There's a lot to be said for being aware of what my body and mind are telling me, so it's at least a step in the right direction. If this is what it takes to continue healing to the person Charlie wants me to be, I can do that. Maybe then he'll treat me a little better, and I can get back to my strong feelings of "probably love."

I'm doing *something* right because he's starting to come back around. I'll just continue on this track. I'm trying my best to heal, and it could all be a lot worse than having to smell pumpkin pie on my way to it.

Gene

I've sat on a small podium next to this bathroom sink for a while now, and I guess it's fine. My podium is in front of a mirror, but my back is to it, so it's not like I'm staring at myself all day. I'm surrounded by other things I've learned the names of because I pay attention: a pill bottle, a tube of lotion, a cup, some kind of towel, and an arm where the water comes out. I've been here for a while, so there's a good chance I'll never go anywhere else.

I'm still saying I've sat "for a while" instead of "it's the only place I've ever been" because, I don't know, that just feels less permanent. The girl who uses me is called Madison. She's a *woman* instead of a *girl* now, I guess, which is kinda weird. I've been hers since she was a kid so, in a few ways, we've grown up together. I've watched her ripen over the years, her body grow taller, and her maturity bigger—reflected in how she uses me more often. And for longer.

There's my measure of growing up: brushing more. That makes sense to me.

I've been around for most of Madison's big moments—kind of like a childhood best friend. It's not that much of a stretch. I've stayed pretty much the same in all the time I've known her, too, except sometimes I get a new head. Those times are nice, but they're rare. I still buzz at the same speed I did in the beginning—up and down, back and forth—and I do just as well of a job as I always have. I probably charge a little slower than I used to, but that's understandable because I'm not brand new anymore. That also hasn't been much of a problem yet because, like I said, I don't leave my podium in this room. There might be a small dent toward the bottom of my body's shaft and my grip's blue color is probably a little faded, but other than those things, I look basically the same. I'm proud of that.

My name is Gene, and I'm a toothbrush. Before you make the "hi, Gene,"-"hygiene" connection, let me beat you to it. You're not the first person to make that joke, and it's not funny anymore. There are a lot of other objects—junk, in my opinion—sitting nearby on this sink, and they've all said some version of that joke. It's not funny. Get to know me first.

This bathroom is dark most of the time. She comes in and out during the day, but she's always in a hurry, then she's gone again. Sometimes, even when she uses me, the darkness hangs around. For the most part, I like Madison, and she takes good care of me, but it's a little aggravating when she does things like that: she pulls me from my podium, butters me up, and I'm sent to work as usual, except in the darkness. I spend so much of my days with no lights on and I mostly prefer it that way, but I also look forward to when they're on. That bit of variance is nice. I sit in the shadows waiting around for her all day so, you can imagine, it's disappointing when she acts like that. Maybe I'm letting too tiny of a thing get to me.

I grew up in another place from where I am now. It was still a bathroom but a different one. All bathrooms are basically the same, but I can tell one from the other. All I do is sit here looking at the room around me, so I pick up on any change—even small ones—in my universe. I grew up in a large one with lots of extra space for her to grow, dance, throw a fit, and spin around. Anything she wanted to do, that bathroom had a lot of room to do it. The counter I sat on was clean, the room was bright, and we were happy.

Then, darkness. But the *pure* kind, with nothing in the background. I was captured and carried away, but I just didn't know to where. And that not knowing was the most stressful part about it. The next time I saw the light was in a different, smaller bathroom that I've never loved, not particularly. But this is Home—my new home.

My setting may have changed, but our routine stayed the same. I see her the same amount of time every day, and we do all the same things, but our background is just different, smaller, and without as much space to spin around. But it's no matter; my work in this new space isn't as different as I thought it would be. There's less for me to stare at, but it's not so bad.

My favorite part about being a toothbrush, no surprise, is when I'm working. I guess it wouldn't be impossible if I preferred to sit on my podium in the dark, but I don't. I *crave* the action. Our routine is this: she takes me from my podium, butters my hairs with some kind of mint-tasting paste, and splashes me under water. Then, I dive headfirst into another darkness.

The second dark is the kind that's full of energy with only a few cracks of light. I know what to anticipate with this darkness because it's the same every time: I'll be set to spin, buzz, and pump against two whole rows of teeth. There have gotta be a hundred of them, at least. The teeth are hard and feel like tiny rocks set in rows. Tiny, white rocks that chomp and grind against each other all day long.

Even with the mint-flavored paste, my work in her mouth always kinda smells bad. Stale. She moves me in there for a couple of minutes so I get a chance to scrub and coat her teeth clean, then she pulls me back out. She'll run my head under water one more time, wipe the drips from my body with a cloth, then set me back on my podium to dry. That part is nice because my body is still buzzing from the work—in a different way than the literal buzzing of when I'm working with the paste. This second buzzing is different, more dreamlike.

Her rocks (teeth) are all basically the same, and I feel lucky I get to mess with them so much. They're set in two rows, one on top and one on bottom, and they curve inward so they'll all fit. The rocks in the front are a little bigger than the rocks in the back, and there's my preference: I like the full, big teeth more than the short, ground-up ones because there's more of a job for me. My time on the smaller teeth is quick. Unexciting. I think she knows that, too, because she pushes me hard into them while I brush, which makes the teeth get bigger. It's slow going, but it's happening. The two of us are a team.

I don't know if those rocks are alive or not. Honestly, I don't know. You'd think I'd have an idea of how much time I spend on them, but they don't do much besides sit there and take it. I've heard what I think is an *eghhh* sound when I brush the bigger guys in the front, but I can't be sure of anything. If they are alive, the two in the top's middle are the most vocal. They're usually the ones who make the noise—of pleasure or pain, it's hard to tell. I assume the noise is good because the paste is minty and they have a bigger surface area to feel my massage, but I don't know because I've never been a tooth. I can't pretend to know what that feels like, or if they can feel anything at all.

Normally, I'm the only toothbrush she keeps, but sometimes, I have company—not sitting on the podium with me but standing in a cup nearby. It's another brush, green in color, and it's a skinnier, more basic version of myself. She calls herself Susan. A man comes in to use her a few times before Madison will move it somewhere out of my sight. It's never very long until he brings her back in for another session of brushes, though, so I'm not as lonely as you might think. Susan hasn't said much more than "hi" and "Susan" because she's shy, I guess, but just having another toothbrush there makes the time pass a little faster. The two of them—man and brush—are starting to come around a little more often, but I'm not sure why. It's cool, but I try not to get excited about things like that. It's all too unpredictable.

Another fun part about my work is when Madison leaves pieces of food on and between her teeth for me to sample. I have to believe that's why she does it. And she leaves them all over: wedged in between the rocks; against the pink cushions on their backs; alongside their bottoms; and as a thin, gritty film on their tops. She has been eating some kind of green mush a lot lately, and I've liked that because it squishes easily and usually passes right through her teeth before I get there. That means there's rarely any food left behind for me to mess with. The only way I know she has eaten it is the slight green coloring that stays leftover on her tongue. But that's no problem. Cleaning gunk off her tongue is the easy part.

She eats a lot of that mush, I think to help me out. We're a good team.

For the most part, I'm thankful for the flavors because it's a peek into her life outside this bathroom. Some of the stuck bits can be a hassle, though—especially the filmy, seedy, and gummy ones. That stuff gets lodged—*housed*—in the cracks of her rocks, and they're not easy to buzz loose. Actually, they're my nightmare. She doesn't usually let stuff sit in her teeth for long, but every second they're stuck makes my job harder. If you ask me, every second they're in is too long.

She's giving me more to work with, slowly, because of her pushing and my brushing. It's harder to notice her teeth getting bigger because I see them all the time, but I can still kind of remember how they were a long time ago: smaller, no doubt. Their growth is gradual, like watching paint dry. I heard that expression once when she was on the phone in my bathroom, but I'm changing it up. *Slow, like watching teeth grow.*

The girl and I have the same goal, and we work toward it together. That's the biggest reason I'm so happy with the work I do. I don't think many brushes get to be this hard, so to speak, on their teeth because all they do is glide across and spread the paste. That must be the case with Susan, and maybe it's a reason she acts so timid. I don't just spread; I *push.* I see that as my taking better care because I make sure that minty goodness is received by all. This work isn't for everyone—it can't be. But it feels like I'm where I need to be, doing what I was meant to. I'm good at it, and I'm happy to help out. I may be old, color-faded, and with a dent in my shaft, but so long as she changes out my head every once in a while, I'll brush like I'm a kid again.

I think I'll be around for a while. In fact, I know I will. Especially if she keeps up making those teeth bigger and getting all my paste to them, we'll work together and I'll be around forever. Our progress is gradual—like watching teeth grow—but we're moving in the right direction.

Tuesday, February 25

People think my having obsessive-compulsive disorder means I have a bunch of hygiene and cleanliness-related compulsions, but it's so much more than that. There are some things I do that could label me as *obsessed* with cleanliness and purity, but also maybe not. Maybe I'm a normal amount of mindful.

By contrast, I'm actually *unclean* about some things: my clothes are haphazard in my dresser drawers, my bathroom counter is littered with rubbish, and sometimes I track dirt through my foyer. I'm a *normal* amount of mindful, and I can be a *normal* amount of messy. Since moving out of my parents' house, though, I'm trying to be better about that last part.

Dr. Ferguson diagnosing me with OCD explained my attention to detail, my over-occupation with being wasteful, my need for things to be "right," my ripping, and my brushing. I could go on-this list is long. The diagnosis didn't explain all my *things*, but it's definitely a better fit than ADHD. Perhaps there lies the differentiation between my *Madison-isms* and my *OCD things*. This has all been a lot of getting used to. I'm making the effort, but it's just a lot.

For the most part, I wouldn't call my routines "compulsive" or "obsessive." But there are a few things I go the extra mile for. I change my bath towel at the end of nearly every day and I keep a different towel to dry different parts of my body, but those are more of my preferences than anything else. I'd be *okay* to use one towel on my entire body for two consecutive days, but I just like to be clean. If hotels change towels after almost every use, it's not a big deal for me to do so, either. I grind my back teeth sometimes when I'm agitated-a common manifestation of OCD-but that could also be a side effect of my medication. I'm aware that I do it, at least, so I can sometimes stop myself. I don't think teeth grinding is anything remarkable.

My diagnosis gave me a new perspective on some things. I now recognize that my oral care, for example, probably crosses over to being an *OCD thing*; I used to brush, and brush, and brush them, many times a day, and with force. I changed my toothbrush's head every six months or so, and I would push my toothbrush very hard across my teeth because I thought I was giving them a better clean. It wasn't uncommon to spit a dot of blood with my rinse. In my mind, though, spitting blood was a win because it meant I was taking away my plaque's chances of hanging on. I flossed until my saliva turned red, and I pushed my brush for two and a half minutes, a minimum of three times a day. I wasn't messing around. I actually grew fond of that metallic-y taste of blood because it meant I was doing a "good job."

I thought I was doing everything right and taking the best care of my favorite asset. I visit the dentist twice a year for a deep cleaning, which is the appointment I've only just come back from. This time, though, he didn't praise me like he usually does at those appointments. I'm stressing out a bit. And Dr. Ferguson told me to write in this journal when I'm wound up. So, here I am.

When the dentist finished his exam of my teeth, he looked at me gravely and said something like, "Madison, you're brushing your gums away. How hard do you push?" I stared back at him in lieu of an answer and maybe nodded my head once, small-like. "If you don't let up, they'll be gone. And gums never grow back." He must have seen the alarm bells ringing in my head. One more jab: "You're also brushing away your enamel."

My alarms rang loudly. I guess taking out my gums and enamel is in the fine print of oral care because I was entirely unprepared for that consequence. I thought I was doing everything right. I eventually got around to reading that fine print, but not without him pointing it out to me. And not soon enough to save some of myself.

"Got it." I was playing *cool* but in a different way. I put my head down and closed my lips tightly as I stood up from the exam chair. "Thank you, Doctor. See you in six months."

The damage is done, and there's nothing I can do about it, except be better. And I am, I'm trying to be: I brush my teeth only in the morning and at night now; I use gentle hands when I floss, and I try not to push so dang hard. I can't reverse the damage done, but I try to compensate by eating softer foods, ones less likely to get stuck between my teeth and ones full of antioxidants. I read on the internet that antioxidants help. I can make some changes to compensate for the damage I've done, but I only needed to be aware of my damage. Glad I am now. With his words "*never grow back*," I'm trying to reset how I think and act on my teeth. It's a strong effort, but a little late.

A lot about this disorder is about my mind over the matter. At least that's *my* approach. I don't want to depend on medication for the rest of my life, so I'm replacing and supplementing with the things God gave me. My ultimate goal is to heal myself *naturally,* but I'm not completely opposed to accepting some help when I need it. I want my healing fast-tracked. For Charlie. My approach might be a little all over the place while I figure out what works for me, but that's just the tradeoff.

I don't think taking a pill for the rest of my life is necessary, so I'm pushing back. I want to do this *my* way. A few things-the caffeine and the meditation, maybe-might be a giant waste of my time, but I'm ready to travel every natural, inborn avenue I can manage. Until I can no longer manage it.

I like to think of what I'm doing as a *slow resistance.* I know at some point my disorder will need my full submission and I will give over to it eventually, but I'm still holding tight to the concept of *normal.* Now, while I'm still young and my mind is still settling into its chaos, though, I'm fighting this disorder on my own terms. Changing around my diet a bit and an active rerouting of my brain will, in theory, weaken the grip that OCD is trying to take on my mind. I intend on fighting this. I'm not sure if I'm going to win, but I'm certainly going to try.

Writing this out does make me feel a little better. One point for Joan.

Mako

I used to be the total package, but then she sliced me in two.

Before all this, my body was double the size it is now, and I didn't have a chasm in my belly. I looked better back then, more put together, instead of the mess I am today, which consists of a portion of soft green and brown mush uncased in a harder, brown shell—my "skin." And with lots of protein. As I am now, though, I'm awkward. Uncomfortable. Before I was sliced, I sat in a green bowl on the counter and watched the world happen around me. I had some privacy back then, at least. Now that she cut me open, there's no trace of that anywhere. Being intact meant my belly was hidden from everyone, and my complexion was a mystery. Now that I'm open, though, everything is different. Everything.

All my memories of the time I was closed in my skin are fond. My life was easier back then because I didn't have to deal with any of the nonsense I do nowadays. Now that I'm sliced open, I'm on display for everyone to see and at all times. It's humiliating, genuinely. By the nature of me, I was pretty sure I'd be cut open someday. So I wasn't *surprised,* really, when I was. But that didn't make it any less miserable.

My name is Mako, and I'm an avocado. Well, I used to be. I don't know what to call myself now, all cut in half and without my egg.

I didn't think I'd ever have to explain this next part to anyone, the one where she cut me in two. Or, rather, I didn't think I'd *get* to explain this part. I've sat alone in my experiences since day one, and that has been isolating. I've been lonely, but I guess I just didn't realize how much so. Now that I finally have the mic, the stress of it is catching up to me. But here goes nothin':

The trauma of my carving started sorta quickly, but the whole procedure also felt very slow and meticulous. A combination of pain and shock does that, I guess. I remember sitting on the counter during what I think was the afternoon, and I was feeling okay about myself. I didn't have a reason to think about my next step, so I never did. I was living fully present in every moment, and life was easy.

Now, I look back on that afternoon as my last peaceful one. It started quickly: first with her hand unexpectedly at my side to lift me out of the bowl, then it's rolling me once around, and finally, it's setting me down again. But the energy was different. I knew enough to guess what was about to happen.

I had about two seconds of rest before her hand came back—this time to my head—and it flipped me to my side. My position and my uncertainty meant that I couldn't have been more uncomfortable. Or, at least, I didn't *think* I could. I was so naïve.

The next minute was a blur: the edge of a knife's blade showed up at my side, close to the fattest part of my midsection. My fear swelled up in the seconds it pushed against me because I could hardly register what was going on. It was the scariest thing to ever happen to me, but not a lot of scary things have happened. I'm an avocado.

The blade held still for a couple more seconds, lightly pushed me for a few more, then broke through. My skin is thick, remember, so it takes a push and sometimes the knife's tip to break it. There's no such thing as accidentally penetrating an avocado and, rest assured, she knew what she was doing. She rammed the tip in to slice through my skin and the first two inches of my insides. The penetration, be no mistake, was excruciating.

"Excruciating" is the strongest word I can think of, but it still feels lacking somehow. The only grace I received was that the pierce of my initial cut was so sharp, it sent me into a kind of cloud above it all. I wasn't totally mentally present for the second half of the cut or, really, anything that came after. Call that a defense mechanism. Dissociation. *My cloud.*

After the blade made its first slit through my side's skin, it did get easier. I still felt an impossible bite as it rolled through my flesh and broke open the remaining skin on my sides, but that pain didn't hold a candle to her initial cut. Remember, I was in my cloud. I don't think I would have made it through without my cloud.

The blade sliced through my skin and the first inches of my green flesh until it hit the egg at my center. The egg I keep inside is like a shield, but inversely so; it's the last stop after my guts are already sliced and spread. If it were on the outside, though, I'd be impenetrable. Saving my egg for last is kinda useless, but I guess it's better than not having anything at all.

Once the blade hit my egg, it wobbled back and forth like drawing an outline, then slid past. Judging from how she navigated around it, my egg may have been a surprise; she may not have known I was keeping it in there. See? *Privacy*.

The knife moved past my egg and cut clean through me. Almost. When she pulled the blade completely out, a small piece of my skin was still hanging to connect my two sides. That didn't faze her anything like you'd think it would, though. She held my halves in each hand, twisted them away from each other front to back, and ripped me apart. She severed my body completely into two pieces and I felt, in all respects, crucified. I don't know how I'm still around to tell this story, honestly.

My body was in two pieces, but my egg stayed with me—on my side—when I was ripped in two. So that made me feel good. I got to keep a little piece of Home. For a few seconds, at least.

Nightmares go on.

She set my first half on the counter, picked up a spoon, and dug a shallow hole in my flesh with its edge. It all happened so fast that I hardly had a chance to register what was going on. She dug into my soft flesh with its tip like she was looking for treasure. Who knew a *spoon* could be so barbaric? She kept jamming it in and moving it around with tiny upward shifts until I figured out what she was after: my egg. She wanted it out, and she gouged into my body until she got it.

She popped it out, which was no small price for me to pay. In the wake of her effort, she left my otherwise smooth, green insides mushed and smashed together. That's not even to mention the feeling of my egg leaving my body; it was like my wind was sucked out. It was painful, sure, but more than that, it was uncomfortable.

My egg popped obediently out and landed in her hand, where she held it in the air like a trophy. *The disrespect.* I saw some of my guts still hanging on it, which made me sick. And there we have my last clear memory; my recall starts getting fuzzy at about this point, either because of the trauma or that sick feeling. I was struggling to focus on and stay present for my slaughter since that first penetration but, once I saw my disembodied egg, *forget it.*

My cloud was my defense mechanism, remember, and my body growing numb was playing the same part. I remember every detail of her scooping my egg out, though, because losing that piece of myself was the most upsetting and unexpected of all this, even more than the slicing. Taking my egg from me felt personal. My naivety kills me.

But not literally. She tried to beat me to it.

In hindsight, the pain of her scooping was nothing compared to what was about to go down. Take my egg, take all the eggs I'll ever have if it'll save me from the fate of my other half. I thought that side might get out easy when I saw it laying on the counter, but *oh,* I was wrong. And I watched it all. I didn't mean to, but I saw everything.

With the same spoon she used to scoop me, I watched as she dug its tip into the flesh of my other half to gouge its guts—my guts—onto a plate. With that same spoon, she scooped a giant glump of green, then doubled back to scrape at my inside walls until all of it was in a stupid pile in the plate's center. First the cutting, then the mind games, then the scooping.

It was appalling. Horrifying. Abominable. *Torture.*

At least, I think it was. I'm separated from that half, so I can't feel what she feels anymore. I can only assume how unpleasant the whole experience was. I'll never be able to ask her, either, I don't think, but I guess there's a chance the scooping felt good. Like a massage? I doubt it, but maybe.

I watched the scene for a long time—until I couldn't anymore. Well, I *could* have. But I chose not to. I needed to stay mentally strong for my time waiting on that counter, and watching the slaughter of my other half wasn't helping.

Telling this story back doesn't feel as liberating as I thought it would. It's actually making me feel worse.

Maybe I've just come into this too fast. I'm aware of that, at least, but the heartbreak of today has been taking up a lot of space in my mind. Excuse me. I'll start over.

I'm an avocado, like I said, and I'm right now perfectly ripe. Physically, I feel good. Mentally is a different story because of what I saw, but I otherwise feel good about myself. I'm confident in how I look, and that's probably why she took my egg and gutted me to death. But I'm not talking about that again.

My insides are a pure, light green, and they have been since she sliced me. While I watched all that was happening, I grew a small brown spot near my top. That growth might have something to do with my sitting so out in the open like I am or, more likely, from all the stress I've been under since being cut. I'm not sure. The brown spot is my least favorite part of myself, but I don't have much to complain about. I'd choose a brown over being scooped out and slapped on a plate any day.

A small, faint buzzing has started on my body—the body half that I still have, at least. The buzzes are concentrated in tiny areas on my green surface, and they're not annoying, not really. I don't know what the buzzing means, but I don't mind it so much. So long as it stays in my background. It doesn't feel bad or uncomfortable, and I'm using it as a distraction to help pass the time and think about something else. The anticipation of what'll happen next is stressing me out so much, and I think it's making the buzzing come quicker.

Maybe losing my egg and some buzzing is as bad as it'll get for me, but I've seen enough to know that's probably not true. Something is coming, and my little bit of hope for something *good* is just about gone. I know better because I've seen worse.

Suddenly, almost as suddenly as the blade showed up at my side the first time, she grabs me off the counter and brings me back into the threat of my situation. It's like she was listening in on my uncertainty, then showing me the worst outcome. The buzzing spots really *have* been my distraction because her return leaves me shaken, literally and figuratively. I had hoped taking my egg would be the worst of what was coming for me.

"Ah, shoot," she mumbles and holds me close to her face. She stares at my green (and brown) for two more seconds before we're back in motion, thumping across the room to the same place I saw my other half gutted. It feels like it's my turn, and a very small part is still holding hope that'll be a massage. I allow myself that little bit of hope because I still have a little bit of spirit left.

BOMP.

Just as abruptly as the first cut—as if it's her signature move—she drops me into a shadow can and onto a pile of only heaven knows what. So that's where I am now, as I'm telling you this. It smells really bad, and I'm set lopsided on the pile I fell onto but, actually, I'm embracing it. I've seen how it can be worse, and I'd choose this smelly darkness over being gouged to a second death.

The can opens wide at the top, and there's enough light for me to see what's around: mostly empty cartons, napkins with stains on them, and some torn-up papers. The last time the light came on, I saw what I think is the skin of my other side. I need the light on to be sure, but I don't think that's something I'd easily mistake. I didn't see my egg lying anywhere nearby, but that's okay. If I can figure out how to move over to my skin, the egg probably won't be far off.

I hope I'm right about all of this, and I think I am. I've been a little out of sorts since the split, and I think rejoining with my skin will help. Maybe the piece that connected us will grow back, and I'll be whole again. My fleshy guts are long gone so I'd definitely be lighter, but I'd be whole again. I'm lonely, and I miss the company of my skin more than even I miss my privacy. I have a lot of questions about what I watched her go through, how it felt, and how she's doing. I want the gang—the two of us—back together.

But I'm alone. Or at least I feel alone. I'm on top of, next to, and partly underneath all kinds of garbage that I don't recognize: a pear-shaped and glass ball with dark wires inside; a short, plastic tube with a circular brush on its top; a wide-mouthed jar with bits of orange wax lining its bottom; and a hundred more things that I can feel, but don't have enough light to describe them in detail. The smell of this box—of all of *us*, I guess—isn't something I can get used to. And I'm not even sure I want to. The smell is getting worse the longer I'm in here. I'm light-headed. My skin isn't far from me, so I have a direct view of it from where I'm lying. If I can't figure out how to move around, though, it might as well be ten miles away.

I'm still buzzing, even a little bit, and I can feel my flesh getting softer. I think those brown spots are somehow turning me into goop. The buzzing might be what it feels for the brown to take over, but I don't know if that's right. And if it is, I don't know what I can do about it. I don't even know if I *want* to do something about it. I expect I'm covered by them—the brown spots—at this point. I don't feel confident in myself anymore, and I don't feel like the green, ripe avocado I used to be. I feel sloppy, I'm stuck in this stinky can, and I'm unable to reunite with the only thing I've ever known: me. A white fuzz is starting to grow on the tip of my forehead, and it doesn't have good energy.

I just can't believe how quickly I've gone downhill. When I was still whole and sitting on her counter, I was confident in myself and in what was happening to me—gruesome or not. Now that I'm here, like this, everything is unfamiliar. I've lost my edge. Or I'm *growing* my edge, depending on how you look at it. I've run out of hope of ever getting back to the bright, fresh air outside this dark can, but I still have some left for reuniting with my skin. That's just how I feel.

I guess this is what happens: some of us are gutted and slapped, and some are dropped into a dark, putrid container. Between the two of us, myself and my other half, I got both. Maybe I should be grateful? I'll work on that.

Monday, March 2

I'm doing everything I can think of to fix myself and my disordered mind, and it's starting to be overwhelming. I don't feel healthy, not yet, but I'm crawling my way back to the top. Slowly, but it'll be worth it.

Maybe not having Charlie so much in my foreground is serving me well.

Maybe I'm better off without him.

Maybe being friends with Rosemary is enough.

My living alone and Charlie keeping his distance means that I have a lot of time to myself these days. I've used it to research more on my disorder, on relationships, and how they can coexist. Specifically, "how to live with it," "how to manage them," and "is it worth it."

Everything I've read points its finger toward my confidence. More specifically, how my insecurities and shortcomings result from my lack of it. How I used to have it, how I lost it, and how I'm trying to get it back. I've learned that I need to work on raising my confidence first, so I can get myself back to neutral.

I'm doing everything I can think of: I wear mascara-even when Charlie isn't around-to feel better about myself; I drink caffeine to slow down my OCD symptoms so he won't notice them; I write down my feelings-usually about Charlie-to help me process; I put in the effort to strengthen all my relationships, like with Rosemary; I eat healthier and I watch my numbers so I'll look good for Charlie and so my disorder won't get the best of me, and I keep this journal because Dr. Ferguson said it'll help with my stress. And because I have nothing to lose.

The hardest change of all these changes is paying more attention to what I eat. Now that I'm living alone and mostly without accountability, it's easy to loaf. I don't even bother to make excuses for my malnutrition anymore because no one is around to see my indulgences. My mother used to call me a *garbage disposal,* telling people, "If you don't want to finish that, give it to Madison. She'll eat anything." I was proud of that reputation because it lent itself to a lot of free food that somehow never showed up on my belly-or, really, lack thereof. Thank goodness for a youthful metabolism. But now that I'm older, my digestion has slowed and my world is a lot more complicated than it used to be. Now, I also have Charlie to think about.

Or, I'm *trying* to have Charlie to think about. If only I can make him want me as much as I want him. He has never explicitly told me, "You're a chunk, Madison," but he's a boy, and boys like skinny girls. Don't they? I'm *trying* to change the way my mind works, but I *can* change the way my stomach sits.

Whether for him or for my own destinations, I have a reason to treat my body well-like a temple, as God designed it.

Saying this another way: where I used to eat pancakes for breakfast and some sort of fried cheese for lunch when I was living in my parents' house, now I'm eating boring stuff like old-fashioned oats for breakfast, nuts for a snack, and a fish or lean meat for dinner. Give or take a banana, spinach where it fits in, avocado by the spoonful, or some kind of "junk" to fill the gaps. It's not the "gummy bear and Little

Debbie" junk it used to be, but it's the kind that I call "junk" because it's bland. Unexciting. The kind that makes people roll their eyes. Cottage cheese with cinnamon, celery sticks with cream cheese, or frozen fruit with peanut butter. Please believe that *I* was the first person to be rolling my eyes at that stuff. But then I grew up, a wrench was thrown into my mix, and now, I prioritize. I want Charlie more than I want Little Debbie.

My healthy eating goes through phases, and right now I'm stuck on avocados.

That's probably the lamest sentence I've ever written, but here I am. I'm grown, and I'm *lame.*

I eat an avocado once a day, give or take. My recipe has it filled with black beans for extra protein, but I could eat it by itself. I really could. I eat six or seven a week, but I only buy three at a time because I can't stand the thought of them turning brown. That's why I only buy three: I'll throw it in the trash with its first hint of a brown spot-with no hesitation, I'll pitch it-and that's wasteful. My mother taught me better than that, and my job doesn't pay me enough to be wasting food.

I know I can get obsessive about some things, but at least I recognize it. I'm obsessed with not eating the brown or mushy spots on my avocados. There, I said it. This obsession falls in the same category as my Expiration Date Mania on milk gallons but, again, I don't think it's necessarily a bad thing. This level of awareness might even be *normal.*

I can't get away from my obsessions and compulsions. I just can't. When I eliminate something from my routine because I feel myself becoming excessive about it, something else pops up. Obsessive-compulsive disorder feels like I'm being chased-and outrun-by my own mind. When I make changes to trick my mind into normalcy, I might maintain the status quo for a day or two before I'm back to obsessing and compulsing about something new. I can't trick myself into being normal for just that reason: I can't trick *myself*.

I never thought I'd be the kind of person who'd have to deal with mental illness, but I am, and I'm doing what I can to push it into my background. As I get older, my health, relationships, and life are becoming so complicated that it's sometimes hard to keep up. I'm trying to keep the balls in my court, though, so I'm trying to normalize-to myself and to other people-whatever comes my way. It's never-ending, really, but it'll be worth it when my life gets back to order.

Sunday, March 8

Charlie called me yesterday afternoon, and he wanted to "hang out." His words. I think that means he wants to try again.

I'm guarded, and I'm hopeful.

I accepted his invitation to dinner and a movie, and I accepted his invitation to pick me up. At six, at my apartment. At least I started the game on my turf.

I didn't get as excited as when we met for coffee because that whole experience left me feeling a little salty and a little more turned off by him. I didn't call Rosemary to do my makeup, I wore the same jeans and t-shirt he has seen a hundred times, and I tried not to think twice about it. I did, though. I thought three and four times about every ingredient of the night. But I tried.

Charlie rang my doorbell, and I waited fifteen to twenty seconds before opening the door. To make me seem less eager, I guess? I don't know. He didn't seem to notice when he stepped right inside.

"I brought pizza," he said, unnecessarily. The giant pizza box in his hands was the giveaway.

"Oh," I said. "Thank you."

I thought our plan was to go somewhere else to eat, which would give me Control over what I was eating and how much. His pizza "surprise" was sweet-he thought it would make me happy-and I played excited as best I could. I faked it, but not well enough.

"What's your problem?" Charlie asked. He might have been embarrassed, shocked, disappointed, whatever, but they all manifest as anger with him. He rolled his eyes to the side and shot a puff of aggravation from his nostrils. "Do you not like pizza now?"

Honestly, I never really liked it. I just don't have a reason to fake that I do anymore.

We argued, he yelled, then we ate in silence. His three slices and my half of one. He didn't notice my small portion or my feigned bites because he was aggravated with me, so I got away with it. Pizza is okay, but it doesn't fall under my health-minded-disorder-diet regime. Every bite of processed food sets me further from my goals. Or, that's what the internet said. Charlie wouldn't understand any of that, or even try to. I nibbled at a piece to make it last a long time. So he wouldn't notice.

After dinner, I picked out a silly, fun movie to lift his mood. I guess it worked because he held my hand for the entire first half. I feel hopeful for the first time in a while. As much as Charlie admonishes me and makes me second-guess myself, I want him to like me. I want that ball in my court, then *I* can decide if I want *him*.

After the movie finished, Charlie claimed to be "too tired" to sleep over at my place, but that didn't make a lot of sense. Feeling "too tired" to *sleep* doesn't have any logic. It's okay, though, because I wasn't expecting-or hoping, really-for him to sleep over. He went home around 11 p.m., which was also fine. I was feeling kind of weird about the pizza fake. I was also very hungry by that point, so I didn't fight his excuse too hard.

As soon as the door closed behind him, I slid over to the microwave to warm up a lean-cut burger and mash avocado to top it. Charlie doesn't try to understand what's going on with me, so it's better if I keep some things to myself. Like my diet.

I look forward to when I won't have to worry about any of this, when my mind is healed, and I'm back to *normal.* I just need some time and patience from Charlie. Either that, or I'll just keep those parts hidden. This is all so much effort, but I want my *normal* back. I want to feel the way I felt before all this, and before Charlie made me feel like such an outsider. Something has to change, and I'm the only one trying to make it happen. That part still kinda irritates me

Lacey

I'm glad I was the one chosen to tell my story because I'm special in a way the others aren't. I'm used a lot, and I'm one of her favorites, so I can speak to what *really* goes on in here. In the bathroom. The timing of this is good, too. Stuff is happening.

Before I get to that, though, I'll introduce myself. My name is Lacey, and I'm like a diamond in a dirt pile. Depending on what stage I'm at in my laundering, that expression hits the target way more than I'd prefer.

I'm made of high-quality Pima cotton, which means I'm softer, thicker, and more absorbent than many of my peers. I'm dark blue, and my color has only barely begun to fade. I'm in my prime right now—at the top of my game—and I feel good. I'm proud of my work, and I care about who I work for. Madison. I've grown fond of her, and I think it's mutual.

I don't remember anything about being made—woven—at the factory, but I remember the whole time I was in the department store. Every second of it. Think about it this way: I was *born* at the factory and *grew up* in the store. Under those fluorescent lights, my memory started, and I grew into every bit of who I am today: an old hand, as it were.

I spent most of my childhood on a shelf at the bottom of a small stack of three or four others. Their weight felt like ten on top of me, but I'm fairly sure it wasn't more than four. I remember they were restrictive and heavy, and I was hot. All the time. My days on that shelf blended into one, save for the big lights turning on and off to mark the start and the end of the day. I had no other way to measure the passing of time and hardly anything else to distract me. Spending all of every day in a department store is just about as fun as it sounds: not very. At all.

There aren't many stories I can tell from my time in there. Life was simple, and I was bored. Hot and bored, all the time. And only heaven knows how long I lay there, waiting. The near-continual stimulation of people and activity around me might make you think it'd be interesting and not so dreadfully monotonous, but it wasn't. People aren't as exciting as I thought they'd be. Or being a bath towel isn't as fun as you'd think.

I remember everything about the day I met Madison, though. I was on the shelf underneath four other towels, all dark blue and soft like me, but I somehow didn't feel a likeness to any of them. For some reason of fortuity, she reached to the bottom of our pile and pulled me from the others. I don't know how I feel about fate or a higher power, but I believe someone was looking out for me that day.

I remember the soft cushion of her hands against my corner when she grabbed hold and slid me out from the bottom, and I memorized the feeling of her snuggling me tight to her chest. It felt *right.* I remember her clean smell, and I can still hear her soft moan when she held me close. She picked me from the bottom of that pile because she recognized I was better than the others on top, and because we had a connection. She understands me, and that's why we're for each other. That's why I love her.

I didn't know it at the time, but that would be my last day on that aisle and my last moments under those lights. I've been here, in her bathroom, ever since. She puts me in the Machine every couple of days, but I'm not counting that time because it's quick, and it's just something I need to do if I wanna hang here. This place also has a light that flips on and off a lot, but this On isn't as harsh as the department store's *on*, and the off doesn't necessarily mean I'm alone. Sometimes, she comes around when they're off, and she has even used me when they were off before. That time was a deviation, but a fun one.

I love this girl and I love hanging in her bathroom, so I don't mind the darkness or the Machine trips so much. I think of those things as just part of my job, and maybe even things to make me *better* at my job. True or not, my perspective is what makes my days go by easier. In a big way, my happiness depends on my perspective. I'm just trying to be the master of mine.

For the most part, Madison is the only one who uses me. And I'm one of the few she uses. I don't want to sound conceited, but I'm her favorite. That feels good.

There's a lot of nudity in this work, and I really don't mind it, especially hers. I even prefer it. I hang on a rack in her bathroom, so nakedness is around me most of the time: while she's getting ready, using the toilet, taking a shower, changing outfits, and all the nudity in between. We trust each other; we can be comfortable, and that's why this works. She's happiest when her clothes are off, and all I want is for her to be happy. I guess, in another way, I'm saying, "*All I want is for her clothes to be off,*" but that's a bit much. You can see what I mean, though.

She hangs other towels on the rack next to me, but I'm the one who cares about her most. It's good to have the others here for company, even if we don't talk very often. Just them hanging there means I'm not completely alone in my experiences. This would all be more tiresome and distressing, maybe, if I hung alone. They're here to make my days pass by faster. She uses us all to dry something different, too, so I think it makes her happy that we're all hanging around. And her happiness, I reiterate, is my priority.

I haven't explained what I do yet, not in any detail. Let's get into it.

A bath towel is . . . or really, *I am* meant to absorb all the wet—in our case, the water—from whatever it comes into contact with. The wet that contacts *her.* All of us can be used on any part of her body, so she switches us up mostly every time we're hung. Once we're hung and for the whole time we're up there, though, we don't get reassigned from that part. Still following me? If I dry her chest, for example, there's no chance I dry her legs until maybe next time. A lot about being a bath towel is playing roulette—Russian Roulette if you consider the options.

I'm smaller than some of the others, so I've been lucky with my assignments. Most of the time, she swirls me around on her head. Most other towels are on a rotation of her other parts, but it seems like I've landed on Head Duty. I'm not mad about that, either; not one thread of me feels like I'm missing out on her other body parts. There are some germs and juices that I'd rather not have to mess with. With that in mind, I'll call my smaller size an *asset*.

I do rotate to her face sometimes, but it's less often. I'm medium, which means I'm about the size of two washcloths. In her opinion, it seems, I'm too small to dry off her body's limbs, a touch too large for her face, and just right for the mop of hair on her head. I've dried her body and face in desperate times, but my size makes it kinda awkward for both of us.

I work on her face every now and again, but I think that's her last resort as much as it's my far-from-ideal. That job is nasty: nettling in her loose skin cells, rubbing against her clogged dirt, and loosening her face's films is far from charming. *The farthest.* Her hair can be filthy and there have been some pretty mean knots, but it's a sure upgrade. I'm pretty much exclusive to it now—we agree about that much, at least. I have my size to thank for my good draw.

I'm not *overjoyed* about any of this, not really, but I do realize it could be a lot worse. I've never had to dry her armpit, for example, or her hiney.

Madison is pretty good about not making me hang on my rack for more than a day at a time, rarely two, which is another thing I appreciate about her. *Call that my pampering.* One day's hang typically means she'll use me for one shower, rarely two, and that's about all I want to handle. She showers around once a day, so between drying *her* and drying *off*, I stay busy. I appreciate the busyness because I'd rather be doing something—drying something—than just hanging out.

So we have a good exchange. I don't have a chance to get bored because I'm never in one place for too long, and she gets wiped dry. My short shifts and frequent washes are her way of showing me respect, and it's mutual. I show mine by completely drying the wet when she needs it. Simple, beautiful.

These past couple of days have been busy for us both because she has been around a lot lately. More showers than usual. I think she met someone. This is the "stuff happening" I mentioned earlier. I listen when she talks on the phone in here, of course I do, and I heard her talking to someone called Charlie last week. Talking on the phone while on the toilet is some risky business if you ask me, but nothing bad happened.

I met Charlie a couple days later, so I guess it's good between them right now. I didn't just *meet* Charlie, either, but I was *all over* Charlie: he took a shower and chose me to dry him afterward. So I guess I know him more than she does at this point. It was a little overwhelming.

He's a good-looking person, and he seems nice—aside from using me for his *entire* body instead of just one part. And for the fact that he's not *her*. He chose me over the other three towels on my rack, though, so at least we know he has good taste.

There's your proof that I'm better than the others. Like I said.

There is one more thing about him that bothers me, but it's smaller and more fixable: his follow-through. All flaws are correctable with a little awareness, but they're still flaws.

When Madison hangs me on the rack, it's always intentional. She smashes my folds flat to make sure I don't overlap, and there aren't any corners for the water to grow its mildew. I hate when I mildew because it makes my whole body smell like wet paper. She hates it too, I think, so she's mindful when she hangs me. After drying Charlie's *entire* body, though, he hung me on the rack crooked, with two corners folded into each other, and with more hiding spots than I knew what to do with. Not a good first impression. I didn't appreciate those parts of him, but like I said, it's just awareness. And it's only strike one.

Madison either anticipated that to happen or she sensed something was wrong because she came right in after he left the bathroom and pushed my reset; she slung me off the rack and tossed me straight into the mouth of the Machine. I'm her favorite, I said that, and I think there's some connection between us. We're connected, so we work well.

As for Charlie, that recklessness is still his only strike. And it can be fixed. Our ending was a little rough, but drying off his body let me experience some new textures and parts I never had before—ones that Madison doesn't have. I don't know how to process it all just yet, but I'm glad I faced its challenge. Then, I'm glad I got to go into the Machine right after.

Charlie seems nice enough, but Madison needs to set some rules. From my place in her bathroom, I've seen her roller coaster of high and low moods; sometimes, she bounces in with a long smile across her face, and other times, she comes in for paper to swipe away her tears. A lot of my existence is like watching a reality show, but one with a main character that I've become invested in.

Based on the one phone conversation I heard and how happy she seems when she's on her roller coaster high, I think this guy is a keeper. It's good to see her happy, and I'm hopeful for the two of them. Being as I can't exactly move around or live beyond this bathroom, all I can do is hope he'll look out for her like I've tried to. Or that he'll love her as much as she loves me.

And next time, I hope he'll bring his own bath towel.

Thursday, March 19

There's no way to fix myself, and there's no way to kill my intrusive thoughts. So I killed Charlie.

I killed him, but I didn't plan to do it. Does that count for anything? I eventually made a plan to kill him-I had to if I wanted to pull it off-but our relationship didn't start off like that. I didn't start dating him with the goal of killing him in the end. That's just how it worked out.

When someone dies, people sometimes talk about the "accident" that caused their death, but there was nothing accidental about this one. They'll say things like he "passed away" or he "moved to the other side" to make themselves feel better about the fact that he's dead, but that's worthless. He's dead, gone, and he's never coming back. It might not have been an accident, but that doesn't mean I don't miss him sometimes.

I planned out every detail in my head for weeks, making sure there were no holes that would lead back to me. I played out every frickin' scenario, and I paid attention to every variant. I ran a tight operation and, honestly, I didn't think I would actually follow through with it. Is it bad that I'm proud I pulled it off? No one knows I killed him so I can't say anything in the way of bragging, but I *can* write about it in here. There's another use for this journal, I guess. My esteem lives and will always live on these pages and in my head.

One more point for Joan.

I like Charlie a lot, even after he's gone. I might have even loved him, but now I'll never be sure. I remember the first time we met: in math class during our junior year. I noticed him immediately when he walked into the classroom, and I was forever connected to his smile. It was like a magnet. He was so confident and I, the paper clip in this analogy, didn't stand a chance. I latched onto him that day, and I've never really let go.

The sentiment was mutual, and we flirted a little back and forth, but it never resulted in anything. I never forgot him, though, and I had to wait for another near-decade for the divine intervention-that day at the coffee shop when I all but tossed my hot tea onto his shirt. It was an accident, of course, but not a regrettable one by any stretch. He asked for my number while he pat his shirt dry, and my feelings came rushing back at full speed.

The rest is history. Charlie may have been the closest I'll ever get to the conviction I've seen over and over in movies: the feeling of *knowing*. We were destined for each other, and I felt it. In his case, though, it was his *doom,* not *destiny.*

The turbulence in my mind began pretty soon after we started dating, which was only a week after our collision at the coffee shop. Maybe it had already started on that first day, but it wasn't strong enough for me to notice through my euphoria. The Lord only knows. That week before he asked me out was a blur of my excitement, new feelings, and amazement at how he made me feel. Spending time with Charlie allowed me to experience all the feelings that had triggered my eye rolls and fake barfing in romance movies for as long as I can remember.

The "turbulence" that started tearing us apart was my thoughts-intrusive thoughts-that I look back on now and consider tame. (*Trip him. Pull his hair. Smack his hand.*) They were easier to ignore back then, mostly because they were completely unexpected. For a long time, I was in a strong denial that they even existed. I thought I was imagining things. Which, I guess I was. It's all kind of confusing. I was a long time away from understanding the root of my problem and still months away from my diagnosis.

Imagined or not, the thoughts still scared me. I had never experienced ruminations like those before, and I was mostly surprised my mind could dream up those nightmares. They were random at first and I didn't think I'd actually act on them but, still, I feared my own weakness.

What is the relationship between me and these thoughts?

Why am I thinking these horrible things?

Am I really a monster?

Those were questions that kept me awake at night, lying next to him, trying to silence my head from telling me, *Cover his face with your pillow and hold it until he goes limp.*

It felt like I was possessed by a monster, but that's not who I am. I'm just not. And for a long time, I feared I was having some kind of psychological break. I worried that if there wasn't a mental illness taking root in my head, there could only be one other explanation for my mind's violent carousel: on some level, I must have wanted to do those things to him. On some level, I must have *wanted* to kill Charlie.

But I don't. I mean, I didn't.

The thoughts got worse, quickly, and it was near impossible to ignore them all. I had a hard time even looking at him without my mind asking, *What if you lose Control in one quick motion and end his life? What's stopping you from killing him, Madison? It's not totally out of the realm of possibility.*

They were persistent, and they were paralyzing. I started avoiding activities, all because I was unsure of what might happen. I was discovering a new side to myself in those thoughts, and I was losing sight of who I am-the Me that I know. I couldn't be entirely confident that I wouldn't act on them one day, either, because I didn't know what I was capable of.

At the same time, the thoughts were like a drug-a nightmare I wanted to go back to sleep for. I didn't really want to murder him, and I tried to silence my mind and make them stop, but another, smaller part of me was thirsty for them. Every time I tried to push them down, they came back stronger. Like a sickness. But I didn't let up. I tried to quiet them a lot in the beginning, convinced that I could make them go away if I just tried hard enough.

I repeated silent mantras over and over: *You're a good person; you're not a killer; this isn't real.* I splashed water on my face. I told myself that I might love him, aloud, in my empty apartment. I Google searched "characteristics of a murderer" and compared them to myself, proving that I was not one. I avoided writing down my violent compulsions so they wouldn't have any power. I inspected every detail of my childhood, looking for holes and explanations for why this was happening to me. I read books about the pathology of a killer, and I did everything I could to dissociate myself.

I was dissimilar to every case and every characteristic I read about. I knew I was. But the thoughts wouldn't stop.

They got more wicked, more specific, one last time. At that point, I didn't think they could get any worse. I believed I'd already reached the top. The more time Charlie and I spent together, the louder my mind shouted at me until it was nearly impossible to see him over the noise.

What if you strangle him with your scarf?

Push him into that road of oncoming traffic.

If you hit him hard enough with that bowl, you'll kill him.

It became too much, and it was hard to be around him. But, in a weird way, the harder it was and the more I struggled when we were together, the more I wanted to be in that space. I guess that's how alcoholics and junkies feel. The monsters in my head were strong and loud, but he was my addiction, and I wasn't willing to let him go. It took all my effort to set my mind on Silent. But I kept showing up for the fight.

Inescapably, it seems, my toxic thoughts hit a fever pitch. So I gave up trying to stop them. I accepted that they weren't going to go away; the voices telling me to murder Charlie, a sweet man whom I might have loved, would have to linger in the background of my life. I started to gear myself toward living that way.

Alongside my demons. I was determined to be at peace with, or at least have apathy for, the voice telling me to me *stick a fork in his eyeball* while I sat across from him at dinner; to *grab the steering wheel and drive into that building* while riding in his car on Date Night and to *bite down hard as you can* while his tongue swiggled around my mouth while we made out. It was a challenge, but a challenge I accepted.

I wanted to see how long we could be together, and how long I could last. I really liked him, and I just wanted to see.

The voices in my head became my drug, and they made me feel good. In a lot of ways, so was Charlie. As destructive as the voices were, they offered a small dose of relief, however fleeting, that kept me coming back for more. Maybe for that reason, I stayed with him for longer than I should have. Truly, Charlie was my addiction.

Our relationship was never *stable,* not really. We broke up over and over again. Really, Charlie broke up with *me* over and over again. I came to think of our Off times as a chance to quiet my mind and keep him safe. When he called us Off, I thought of that as his needing a break from me. A break from my mind. In our Off time, I hoped he would reflect on us, then come back to me from a different angle. I hoped he would change his mind about not trying to understand *why* I am the way I am and the reason for my being *too much*. If he would just take a little bit of time to understand me, he would realize the meat behind my *madness*.

Every time Charlie came back around, though, he made the same effort as before we had gone Off: none at all. Still, though, both of us kept trying to make it work. I tried hard.

We were destined and doomed for each other, Charlie and I were. For me, I was intoxicated. I realized I kept him in my life to feed my addiction to him. Or to the challenge of him. I'm still not sure which. Charlie was addicted to me too, I think, but in a different way. Dating me was like dancing under a storm cloud: some days, I was able to tune out my thoughts better than others and he was safe. On my bad days, though, he was in danger of getting struck by lightning. He might have also been addicted to the challenge.

My life is lonelier now that he's gone, but it'll normalize soon. I miss his companionship, having someone to carve pumpkins with and to cook me dinner, but *on my own* is what I'm used to. On the contrary, I won't have to justify my *things* to anyone or share my space with someone who leaves the lights on and the towels crooked on the rack. I'm free to be as *frustrating* or *too much* as I want without someone reminding me of it. I probably would have put up with how he treats me forever-if it weren't for the perspective Rosemary gave me. It feels good to have good people in my corner. And I deserve to. Not only that, I thought our relationship was *normal,* so I changed my life around to accommodate it, to accommodate *him*. I only saw how dysfunctional we were when I started spending time with Rosemary and her boyfriend.

I wanted the love, the respect, and the patience those two had. But Charlie just ain't it. *Wasn't* it.

I didn't plan on killing him for most of the time we were together, at least. I thought I would be able to ignore my turbulence forever and that, someday, it might even stop. I never thought I was capable of hurting someone, much less killing them.

Then, one day, I guess I just did.

About the Author

Kristin Beale is a regular contributor to the Christopher and Dana Reeve Foundation's blog and author of *Greater Things, Date Me,* and *A Million Suns.* She's a sixteen-time marathon finisher, parafencer, and weekly comic strip artist. She resides near Richmond, Virginia.

Printed in the USA
CPSIA information can be obtained
at www.ICGtesting.com
JSHW082122090823
46233JS00001B/12